Tirin Desgjin had everything she wanted, but it took being kidnapped to see it. The romance she dreamed about, the acclaim most worked all their lives to achieve, the belonging she'd always wanted, and the magykal talent that she thought would bring it all to her.

The usual rites of adulthood for Tirin's twentieth birthday bring about more than her uncommon magykal ability: they expose a secret long buried. A secret that forces a cursed elf to face his nightmares, a prince to face his daemons, and a father to face his past. Will Tirin survive all the revelations?

I0683792

Wonderlost
By Antoinette J. Houston
Edited by Bonny Moseley

This story was first written and completed on Wattpad. All characters are totally made up by me.

ISBN-13:
978-1641862820 (Pronoun)

ISBN-10:
1641862823

Other books by Antoinette J. Houston

Urban Fantasy Series
Red Summer – An Urban Fantasy
Wil's Winter – Five Years Later

Space Opera Series
Mostly Human
Semi-Human
Beyond Human

Antoinette J. Houston

CHAPTER ONE

Wonderlost

The waning night was lit by a full moon wrapped in feathery clouds. It was the only light Tirin Desgjin had to illuminate the thin path before her. It was finally spring. Chill bumps rose over her earth-brown skin as a soft breeze whirled about her. Her feet knew the path by heart. For seven years she has made this trek in secret, keeping to the shadows as she leaves the safety of the Elven city of Ao'lean. She followed the path she has created over the years, through the hidden crack in the forbidding gray walls that surrounded the city.

As the clouds gave her brief cover, she quickly made her way across the clearing and into the Forest of guardians. She tried to keep in the scant shadows, hiding from the guards that patrolled the top of the wall.

The forest was made up of ancient trees that encompassed and have guarded Ao'lean for generations with magyk beyond even the elder Elder's understanding.

Tirin made her way northeast, across a field that softly dipped into a vale of spider willows. She carefully moved along the path through the squat, dark trees, hugging her arms against herself within her cloak to make sure she didn't brush up against any of their oozing thorns. The trees only grew three to four feet tall before they spread their prickled branches along the ground like long, vile spider's legs. She had to be careful as their hidden roots would pop up randomly to trip the unwary trespassers just for fun. She had heard they were poisonous, but knew they weren't. She knew firsthand they simply caused a hellish rash.

She continued along the path just beyond the vale and crossed at the shallows of the River Green, silently heading northeast where she would eventually enter Ebon's Woods.

Tirin paused for a moment, hearing something that didn't belong. She stood still as she listened for the sound again. Nothing.

Tirin took a deep breath before continuing forward into Ebon's Woods. Here the pines were like none anywhere else. Their slender trunks were the color of the blackest ink and their leaves were like new silver fresh from the smelter. The story was that a woodsman called Ebon Tryln was killed here almost a hundred years ago. Days after his blood had soaked into the ground where he fell, the trees changed in mourning. It was a story hard to swallow, but no one was ever able to explain why the pines here were so drastically different from others.

After she made her way through Ebon's Woods, a large open field stood between her and a forest even older than the one that protected the Elven city.

Old magyk filled the air here where Tirin's trek would come to an end. A fog would coalesce about her before she made it halfway across the field. Fingers of cool moisture touched wherever there was exposed skin, as if searching. The fog never waned; it thickened when anyone got close to the old forest. The ground itself was alive, convulsing and moving as it saw fit to deter entry. The trees were monstrous, large enough to be converted into homes, much like the one she was using as her workshop now.

Wonderlost was the name of this forest, once home to a hermit sorcerer. His secrets were hidden away in this forest of mystery, at least until Tirin happened across what was left of his partially mummified corpse and his well-preserved compendium several years back.

elsewhere....

Trailing behind Tirin was a large wolf-like animal. It was almost three times larger than the wolves of this region. He quietly watched as Tirin prepared to enter Wonderlost. Camouflaged by his dark fur and shadows, the wolf listened to the strange words she chanted, strange words he knew by heart now after the many times he had followed her here. The wolf retreated a few feet as his body slowly began to change. The pouch he held in his mouth dropped to the ground as his form went from four legs to two. His face receded with the snapping sound of shifting bones and ligaments, all while his size and mass shrank. Fur gave way to skin the color of goldenrod and his wild rave-black mane curled and neatened somewhat. In the matter of moments a male elf stood where the monstrous wolf had been. Tyrus Raylok quickly hid behind a bush. He removed his clothes from the pouch made up of his cloak and dressed while he watched Tirin command the area to heed her. He could feel the ground tremble before it stilled.

Tyrus observed, still in awe after all this time, as the fog dispersed before her. Tirin entered the forest unmolested, the will of this place bending only to her. He had made the attempt to follow her once. Once was all he needed to know that Wonderlost would not allow harm to its new master.

Tyrus remained hidden on the other side of the field, well within the cover of Ebon's Woods. He watched, semi-relieved, as his charge vanished within the ancient forest. Somehow Tirin had gained control of the magyk that warped this place. Regardless of the racial restrictions, magyk had found its way into her life. Humans were known for their ability to create weapons of great destruction, to invent grand mechanical monstrosities to aid in the building or

9

demolishing of cities. Magyk was not a strong point with them; it was something they often shunned.

Tyrus had never thought to question Tirin about her midnight trips despite this, feeling it unnecessary. Despite the scary stories of her kind's reputation with magyk, he felt she could handle it. Having grown up with her, he wouldn't blame her for being vengeful. She had more than a right to become a cruel mage. But Tirin wasn't ruined by her past, their past. All he knew was that she seemed happier when she left in the mornings. That was all that mattered to him. He stared at the thick fog for a moment more before heading over to his usual hiding place where he waited for Tirin to finish her secret business.

He knew that magyk was in her blood. Baelor Desgjin, her adoptive father, had mentioned that her mother had been a Blight witch. He could only hope that Tirin had her mother's willpower and mental strength.

Time passed as he became lost in thought. Night faded into early morning and the night bird calls were replaced with the sun songs of the starlings. Tyrus looked up at the brightening sky. He knew Tirin's life had been hard since being brought here as just a baby. She had struggled, having her mother die so soon after her birth and then having to grow up the only human in an Elven society. Baelor was an elf of high status, but he couldn't protect his daughter from the ridicule she endured growing up. To Tyrus' knowledge, Tirin hadn't told her father about any of her troubles over the years with his people. He honestly couldn't believe that the once highly revered and feared Imperial High guard didn't already know.

Originally, Tyrus had been one of Tirin's childhood tormentors. He and a few others went out of their way to make sure Tirin knew she was not wanted. She had been thirteen when fate had taken a turn for the both of them. Drastically changing the dynamics of their relationship, Tyrus found himself becoming enamored.

As the sun finally began its ascent over the horizon, the diurnal fauna began to awaken. Tyrus loosened his cloak as the morning warmed but his memories, now whirling in his head anew, caused a chill to go through him. What had happened to Tirin seven years ago still disturbed him. He closed his violet eyes as the memory forced him to relive it.

Seven years ago...

It was early afternoon and the city of Ao'lean was alive with springtime activities. Everyone seemed to be in high spirits as the sun gently warmed the day. Everyone, that is, except Tyrus, who strode brusquely away from his home.

The young elf paused, turning to glare back at his mother as she frowned down at him from an upstairs window.

How could she say those things to him knowing how his opinions mirrored those of most of her friends as well? Baelor Desgjin was a fool for adopting a human. Most of Ao'lean thought the old elf a fool for returning at all. He had allowed himself to be turned into a slave for years by humans and then came back here, mutilated and carrying one of their whelps.

Tyrus unclasped the fasteners of his tunic as he gradually warmed up. He pulled his shirt out of his trousers, no longer caring about his appearance. The sound of his boots against the cobblestone was heavy at first, but lightened as his thoughts deepened. His mother knew nothing. To reprimand him for teasing the human girl, telling him to think about his actions. Tyrus scoffed at his mother's words. "Treat her as you would want to be treated." She was human! What did it matter how he treated her? Her father didn't seem to have a clue to what his 'daughter' was going through.

Tyrus paused. Baelor Desgjin was a very observant man, and he doubted that Tirin was able to hide her everyday experiences from him.

Antoinette J. Houston

Tyrus combed his raven curls back, his haughty attitude softening. Despite the difference in blood, Tirin had a lot in common with her father. For one, they were both stubborn and determined to be or do what was necessary. Tirin was an exemplary student regardless of the prejudices of some of the teachers. She had won the respect of many who would rather spit on her than look at her. And regardless of what was done to her, she seldom gave a reaction. Her anger was something rarely seen, but when it surfaced she was almost scary. If it wasn't for her tiny stature, her anger might be taken seriously one day.

He reached a shaded spot beneath a flowering dogwood and sat down on a well-worn bench. The small commons was pleasantly quiet and isolated; it was the usual spot where he and his friends met after school was done. Today was a holiday and he was alone, but he didn't mind.

Maybe what his mother was trying to tell him wasn't such a bad idea. His home was the closest to hers, so he often observed how she did absolutely nothing to deserve the treatment she received. She greeted all her neighbors every morning. Disregarding the rebuffs she was usually greeted with. Determined to remain courteous to everyone.

The only problem was those he called friends wouldn't see it that way. Tyrus regarded his mother highly and to make her unhappy never sat well with him. Nevertheless, Darec Shiey was the son of the High Lord and what Darec thought meant a lot as well. Being friends with the sole heir to a large domain was great for raising one's social status. And in Ao'lean, status was everything.

Tyrus rubbed his temples and looked up in time to spot the Young Lord creeping his way along the great wall that encompassed the whole of the city. He watched as Darec kept deep in the shadows, looking as if he was stalking something...or someone. Tyrus moved his line of sight a few meters ahead of the Young Lord to spot Tirin making her way toward a concealed corner. She was apparently oblivious to Darec's presence as she continued toward an overgrown talak bush. Tyrus got up slowly and moved carefully toward them, his curiosity aroused. He watched as Darec shortened the distance between himself and Tirin. Slowly Darec removed two items from his pocket, a white cloth and a smaller object obscured by his hand. After doing something to the cloth, Darec abandoned his stealthy approach and ran at Tirin.

Tyrus moved faster as he watched Darec place the cloth across Tirin's face. Tyrus' throat tightened as he watched her struggle wildly against Darec for a minute before going limp in his arms. Fear filled Tyrus and forced him to run across the commons toward the Young Lord. Darec and the unconscious Tirin disappeared behind the talak bush before Tyrus was able to get enough breath to yell after them. He paused only a second to retrieve the dropped cloth as he reached the bush. The scent was pungent and familiar, enough that Tyrus didn't need to bring it close. It had the same smell as the sleeping draught used on the High Lord's pampered dog, Tiya, in her last hours before putting her out of her misery. Alarm filled Tyrus and he moved closer to the bush and easily found the large crack that was their apparent exit.

For a moment Tyrus couldn't move. What was Darec thinking? Tyrus looked at the large crack in the supposedly impenetrable great wall of Ao'lean. Eying the thin, foot-worn trail, he figured Tirin had been the sole user of this path to escape her life within the walls of Ao'lean. He swallowed dryly and carefully made his way through the short tunnel. He exited to face the clearing, just barely catching Darec disappearing into the Forest of guardians directly across. He quickly followed, barely finding the path again. Tyrus' concern turned to fear as Darec was nowhere to be found.

The thirty minutes that had passed felt more like eons as Tyrus made his way through the woods. Fingers of fear dug deeper and deeper as there was no sign of Darec's passing anywhere.

Then he heard it.

Antoinette J. Houston

It was a soft moaning alternating with rhythmic breathing, slow at first yet gaining speed. Tyrus moved quietly toward the noises, his heart in his throat. He didn't want to admit that he knew what was going on and tried to block the truth with other possibilities for the noises he was hearing. He finally made it to the small clearing and froze. Hate, fear, and disgust filled him as his heart dropped to his feet.

A small way ahead of him he spotted the Young Lord. Darec's shirt was undone and his trousers were gone as he rocked back and forth on top of the still unconscious and now nearly naked Tirin.

"No." It was to have been louder but Tyrus' voice couldn't seem to find the conviction. Tyrus bolted from the bushes to slam into Darec, sending the Young Lord sprawling.

"What the hell are you doing?" he yelled as Darec jumped to his feet, alarmed and embarrassed. Tyrus removed his tunic and covered Tirin with it while Darec redressed quickly and calmed himself. He actually smiled before retrieving his clothing.

"Tyrus." Darec smoothed the wrinkles and bits of leaves and twigs from his clothing. "You followed me?" The Young Lord raised a brow. "Did you want to do--?"

Tyrus watched, a little confused at first, as Darec's head snapped to one side. He then realized that he had just hit Darec.

Darec remained on all fours in shock and pain. Fear filled the Young Lord as he had never been hit before, by anyone. The sensation it sent through him was more than unpleasant yet strangely exciting.

"Do! Not! Dare!" Tyrus bellowed. "What is wrong with you?"

"Calm down, Tyrus." Darec remained on his knees, shocked at his friend's reaction. "It's not as bad as it—"

"Do you know what you are saying?" Tyrus backed off. "You drugged, then raped her!"

"Tyrus, don't get so worked up. She's human; no one will care." Darec started to smile again and pulled back sharply as Tyrus reached for him. The glare in those violet eyes showed utter disgust.

The last thing Tyrus wanted to do was find himself agreeing with his mother's words, but there was no way around it. Tyrus' mother had said that there was something wrong with Darec and Tyrus had actually stood up for him. To say that he was disappointed would have been an understatement. To have witnessed the act in progress made it so much worse than admitting that his mother had been right. Regardless of how he felt toward Tirin, the thought of doing something like this was inconceivable.

Tyrus raised his fist again, unable to think of anything else, and watched as Darec's amber eyes grew wide with panic.

Tyrus' arm stopped inches from Darec's face and both boys looked at each other in alarm as the breathing of a third was heard. Tyrus watched as Darec peered around him. Darec's throat moved nervously as he swallowed his blatant fear. He knew something unseen was restraining Tyrus.

"You're not supposed to be able to..." Darec whined before being sent flying away from Tyrus.

Tyrus watched as the Young Lord went crashing into a tree and then crumpled to the ground. He wanted to turn and face whoever was doing this, but couldn't move a muscle. All he could do was watch as Darec raised his head, his brown hair falling away to reveal a cut on his forehead.

"How? How could you do this to me?" Tirin screamed from behind Tyrus. Whatever was holding Tyrus released him for a moment only to push him out of the way before being pinned to the ground. Tyrus watched in frightened awe as the small human girl moved forward. Her brown skin gave off a soft bluish glow. *"I have done nothing to you to be treated like this!"* she screamed, the glow brightening sharply. Her dark eyes flashed.

"Tuh-Tirin...Tirin, stop," Tyrus called from his prone position, his concern begrudgingly going from her to the Young Lord as the air picked up around them. Leaves from the past winter rose from the ground and whirled about the three of them violently.

Tirin hugged Tyrus' tunic about her. "I know you hate me for what I am, but to do this..." Her voice trailed off as she clasped her hands over her face and screeched. "You deserve to suffer! To suffer so painfully!"

"Tirin--!" Darec started, only to yell out in pain as something took hold of him and wrenched him from the ground.

Tyrus could only watch, paralyzed, as something seemed to be crushing Darec. "Tirin, do not do this!"

She glared at him. "And you still want to protect him?" she asked, amazed. "Regardless of how you feel about me, I do not deserve this!"

"No, Tirin, you are right, you do not deserve to be treated like this. No one should be treated that way...but for you to take his life you will be destroying three in the process."

"I don't care," she growled.

"You won't be able to continue living in this place you have called home for thirteen years. Sire Baelor will be devastated...he...he will not have his daughter anymore, not the one he raised."

Tirin's glare softened some.

"High Lord Shiey will have lost his only heir and only son, the last reminder of his deceased wife—"

Her glared intensified. "I care nothing for the High Lord's wife or brat!" The wind picked up violently and Darec screamed in intense pain.

"Tirin!" Tyrus yelled

Tirin ignored him, her voice now audibly chanting words he would never comprehend. She was casting spells she shouldn't know and Darec was going to be their very first victim. The whirling wind suddenly began taking on a ghostly form, a translucent serpentine form that made Tirin hesitate. Tyrus became even more concerned as it was apparent that something was wrong. He watched the serpent grow while it whipped around its conjurer then circled Darec, who screamed once before passing out.

Tirin faltered as the dragon circled Darec once more, then headed for her.

"Oh no, I forgot!" She turned to run and disappeared in a whirlwind of leaves as the dragon encircled her. She screamed as if she was being murdered.

Darec dropped from the air and whatever force that had Tyrus pinned to the ground was no more. Tyrus found it surprising that as soon as he was free he was up and running for Tirin.

Everything became silent after the small magykal tempest dispersed. Tirin was laid out on the ground unmoving, unaware of what was around her. Disgust at Darec filled him anew as he saw the bruises flowering on Tirin's face and arms. He turned to face the Young Lord, an insult ready, but the heir to Ao'lean was nowhere to be found. The brat prince had escaped without his knowing. He took only a moment to decide whether to chase after the Young Lord and decided to tend to Tirin first.

"Tirin?" Tyrus called before making his way over to her. He put his hand on her shoulder and the first thing through his head was what he was going to tell Sire Baelor. Was she dead? He swallowed fearfully.

Tyrus put his fingers beneath her nose, but he was shaking too much to tell if she was breathing or not. He gently put his head against her chest and tried to listen for her heartbeat over the thudding of his own. He closed his eyes in relief when her chest rose and fell. He pulled back quickly when she whimpered. Before he could move out of her way, she shoved him, and he landed on his backside with a cry of pain. Her hands went to her stomach as she doubled over. He watched in horror as her stomach grew larger and *larger, almost as if she was going through the phases of pregnancy in a matter of moments. Her cries of pain became louder and louder, and all he could do was sit there and watch until her stomach stopped increasing in size. Whatever she had tried to do to Darec was the cause of this but he couldn't leave her like this. His mother being a midwife, Tyrus remembered a few things his mother did to make the mother-to-be more relaxed. He quickly ripped a bit of his undershirt and wrapped it about a stick before gently putting it to her mouth. "Bite down," he whispered in her ear as he propped her up on his legs.*

"What's ....happening?" she groaned around the stick between waves of pain that racked her body in close intervals. Tyrus swallowed as he held her hands.

"It seems that you are about to give birth..."
***

Present

Everything had seemed so surreal then. Tyrus knew even then that Darec had seen him as only a lackey, but he had hoped it would become more. Whatever the Young Lord said to do, Tyrus and the others would do without question. A lot of it had to do with tormenting the little human girl. Darec seemed to hate her most for reasons only he could understand. No one questioned why or seemed to care much, except for Tyrus' mother.

Briefly Tyrus was blinded by the morning sun as it peeked through the trees while coloring the sky beautiful shades of rose and lavender.

Tyrus sighed as he remembered carrying her back home and then sneaking into the garden at the back of her house. He had left her there, not sure what to do. That day could never be forgotten, but in Tirin's case it had been. Somehow, after that whole ordeal, Tirin acted as if none of it had ever happened.

He looked up in time to see Tirin emerge from the fog of Wonderlost, her business in there now done. Once Tirin had passed his hiding place in Ebon's Woods, Tyrus stretched and proceeded to follow her home, the memory quickly put away.

Tyrus followed Tirin back through Ebon's Woods and then back across the River Green. He watched her pause as she bent to retrieve yet another stone to add to her growing collection of river-smoothed quartz. As they made their way toward Spider Vale, Tirin stumbled and gave off a small scream when she stepped wrong onto loose gravel.

The scream made Tyrus think about his nightmare. It had started four years ago, sporadically occurring until a week ago. Now it was every night. Tyrus looked toward the east. The miserable willows of Noir Swamps were more than several miles away yet clearly visible to his sharp eyes. It was the home of the Witch Bayne, the woman who had changed his life forever in one night due to a failed dare given to him by Darec.

Tyrus looked away from the swamps in the distance to see that Tirin had gotten to her feet and was almost through the vale. She would be safe once she entered the Forest of guardians. His secret assistance was no longer necessary.

Like so many times before, Tyrus reluctantly made his way toward the swamps to confront the witch, or at least attempt to. He could never make himself enter the swamp once he reached it. It had taken a long time to get up the nerve to even make it as far as he had. If it wasn't for the fear that his nightmares could come true, he would never go anywhere near the swamps. But the nightmares were growing worse every day. They were vivid and violent and now showing him attacking Tirin.

He raises her head to kiss her properly. Tirin doesn't refuse him; in fact she welcomes him. Tyrus' happiness is short-lived when she suddenly pulls away from him. He grabs at her hands only to jerk back when he sees they're covered with long black fur. He watches in horror as his transformation spreads from his hands to the rest of his body. He looks up to see Tirin has distanced herself away from him before he falls to all fours. The thing he feared most becomes a reality, as he no longer has control over himself. A feral growl escapes him and the distance between him and Tirin shortens. He can smell her fear when she screams and it only enrages him more. He jumps on her and brings her down quickly. He screams silently to himself to stop before being blinded by a sudden spray of crimson.

A violent shiver shot though his body as the fear of that happening was renewed. The signs were all there that it could. For six years he had been cursed to uncontrollably change from elf to monstrous wolf. He could never hurt Tirin, not of his own free will. Not with the way he felt for her, not with what she's done for him. But the nightmare made things glaringly apparent. All this time he had kept a restraint on his emotions, believing them to be the trigger to his transformation. And for a long time the transformations became less frequent. But in the last year that had changed. He had noticed that his elven features were becoming more lupine. There were aspects of his alter form that had gradually become permanent. He allowed his hair to grow long and wild to hide the noticeably changed shape of his eyes, ears, and face, the ebon claws instead of fingernails, the enlarged canines, and the augmenting of his senses. He feared with all these gradual changes that one day when his curse took over he would lose himself entirely. Thus, he had decided he needed to talk with the Witch, plead with her to raise her curse, forgive him for a childish prank, for he had been punished for long enough.

The thought of confronting her ate hungrily at his reluctant courage. The first time he had visited Noir Swamps was on a dare for Darec. After the incident with Tirin, word of his 'betrayal' left

Antoinette J. Houston

him friendless and miserable. In order to get back into Darec's good graces, he was to retrieve an item from the witch's hovel as proof of his visit. Tyrus couldn't deny the desire to have everything go back to the way it was, but the dare only succeeded in making Tyrus see that Darec was not worth it.

Since the nightmares began, Tyrus had visited the edge of Noir Swamp a dozen times but had never been able to set foot into its darkness, thanks to courage that deserted him every time he attempted to revisit the witch. Witch Bayne cursed him for intruding on her privacy; she wanted no company, no intruders. The old woman may not even remember him after all this time and if she did, she may see his visit as another intrusion and curse him with something worse.

Tyrus sighed and slowly started for the swamps for the thirteenth time.

CHAPTER TWO

Comne

The sun was hanging high in the afternoon sky hours after Tirin's return. The city of Ao'lean was bustling with the everyday sounds of a lively province. Spring brought the promise of new things and changes to the old. There was the sound of happiness flowing through the open window and into Tirin's room. It was a sound that brought a smile to her still sleeping face at first, but then reminded her of the horrible reality that was her life. Today was her birthday. She was now twenty years of age. With age comes clarity, the elders said often.

Every sign of sleep faded quickly as she sat up suddenly. When she was younger she had always dreamt of this day, the day she would show all of her father's people how wrong they were about her. She would be at an age when all the wrong done to her would be forgotten because she would share in a celebration that would make her like everyone else.

The celebration had two parts this year; one was the Comne, the other the Barryn Ritual. The Comne was the equivalent to a mass birthday party, for all of those reaching the legal age of adulthood. Tirin wasn't concerned with that. It was the last-minute Barryn added two weeks prior. The Barryn was the impromptu ritual that awakened inert power or showed you a major factor of your future, good or bad.

The clear noon sky didn't seem so bright as she peered out her window, taking in the colorful decorations that were being put up for tonight. The festive ribbons and flowers wound around the same route as the streets leading toward the center of the city. She could see the tables, the stage for the performers, and the dance area where she dreamed of showing her grace and ability. Then there was the heart of the city, the Dual Gardens, where everything could be taken away from her.

The outer Garden was like another world. Flowers and plants that were long extinct beyond the gates of Ao'lean grew here in the earth that housed roots of the oldest tree in this world. The inner Garden was where the Barryn would take place. Another stone wall at the center of this garden unsuccessfully encircled the ancient tree. Its massive roots and limbs displaced the many times replaced bricks. Now left to the tree's mercy, the inner garden's wall slowly falls to over grown ruin adding to the bewitching ambiance. Tirin let her eyes move up the drab stone wall encompassing the tree she once thought would be her chance to gain the respect and adoration she'd always wanted: the Grand Ao'lean, the namesake of this city.

The Barryn ritual was held when the Grand Ao'lean deemed it necessary to awaken what was dormant or to open one's eyes to a possible future.

It didn't matter what age the receiver was, just whether they were ready. Not everyone summoned by the old tree received anything. But there was only one summoning and there were many never summoned. It just so happened that this year the Barryn would be on a Comne. Tirin had been told all her life that only Ao'lean elves could be summoned by the tree; only those who were born here could receive an audience with the Grand Ao'lean. Tirin looked away from the old tree and then closed the curtains smartly, almost ripping them from their anchor. That old tree was the same as those surrounding the city. It was the same genus as the trees populating the forest of guardians beyond Ao'lean's gates. Their magyk confused those who did not belong, those who were not of this town. Unless guided by a local, they would never make it to the gates or out of the forest. Tirin had never had that problem. Never had the trees used their magyk to prevent her from getting in, but...

Tirin shook her head and moved to her closet. There was no choice; she had to leave. History had no stories of humans with magyk who didn't try to take over the world or mindlessly destroy civilizations. There were only stories of the magyk driving them crazy and evil. Even their deaths were horrible: the magyk built up within them would be released explosively, taking large numbers of people with them. She couldn't stay here and let that happen. She knew they would all want her to leave anyway, or worse, take her out and kill her themselves.

Tirin shuddered.

After freshening up she quietly headed downstairs, carefully taking each step so as not to alert her father. She stood straight at the sudden realization of how quiet the house was.

Where was Tyrus? He was usually up around this time. She reached the bottom of the stairs and looked around, through the dining area, the living room, the library, the den, then the kitchen. Tyrus was nowhere to be found. She eventually realized where he might be. Just as she would make her trips late in the night, he would make a few of his own early in the mornings. She even dared to follow him once, careful to stay downwind of him due to his enhanced senses. For an hour, he would travel at a pace that had been hard to maintain at first but strangely had gotten easier for her to keep. Noir Swamps would be his destination and at the very edge of it would he stand, never entering, sometimes threatening to, but never succeeding. She hoped his absence meant that he had finally entered.

Returning from Noir Swamp, Tyrus howled in utter disgust with himself. To visit and revisit the swamps only to stand there at its edge, staring into its depths instead of entering to confront the human witch, was growing old quickly. Something snagged his cloak as he stormed into Ao'lean Forest and without thinking he turned and attacked the bush that caught him. Without noticing that only his hands had transformed, his ebon claws became evilly hooked rapiers as he blindly ripped the bush apart. When the twigs and leaves settled he covered his face in humiliation.

But he felt better.

Tyrus turned and continued for home, wondering if he would ever be brave enough to confront Bayne. He needed her to remove this curse. He would beg for her forgiveness; nothing would be too humiliating.

He sighed as he looked at his hands, now elven save for his ebon nails, finally feeling the sting of the few scratched he received. Certain aspects of his transformation were a little disturbing. The howl earlier was a surprise to him. He wondered what else was going to change.

The wind suddenly picked up and he found himself watching the path it took. Seemingly starting at his feet, it blew into the brush ahead, then into the glittering foliage of the trees. The emerald leaves of the guardians of Ao'lean, younger versions of the Grand Ao'lean, shimmered like a thousand flash beetles. He observed the surrounding area, still amazed at the blessing most of the elves took for granted. He found it more than a privilege to live within the protection of a mysterious fortune such as these Ao'lean trees. These trees had been studied for hundreds of years and yet their secret remained well-hidden. No one knew how the trees worked, how they came to hold magyk enough to protect a large and still-growing city. He had seen the boundary of the city expand three times and each time the edge of Ao'lean Forrest remained exactly half a mile away from the city's walls. He had often wondered how it was that no other living being could enter the forest without getting hopelessly lost within its magyk. Except for the Ao'lean Elves…and Tirin…even though she was human.

How was it that the magyk of these trees could know that she belonged and other humans or beings did not? This fact brought on more questions: how exactly had Sire Baelor met Tirin's mother, and what had really gone on between them? This was a man who was ashamed of nothing, who dared to return from his captivity disfigured in a way that was considered obscene. The loss of a limb was a weakness that could never be strengthened. He wouldn't say he loved Tirin and continue to refuse her as his own blood if she was. Sire Baelor would not keep such information hidden to himself. Maybe Tirin had been here long enough that the magyk the trees possessed, specifically protected those who lived there, like a certain aura only they could discern.

Tyrus looked up at the bright sky and found himself, with reluctance, remembering that today was of great importance. Whether he wanted to or not, he was required to get back. He sighed, tearing his eyes from the Ao'lean trees, and started back for home.

Tirin grabbed some sweet bread and fruit before heading toward the front door. As she exited, she prayed that a tongue-lashing was all she got when she returned well after the festivities.

"What're you up…" the Young Lord, Darec Shiey, began, startling her and causing the small gathering of food to fall from her hands as she greeted him with wide eyes. She picked up her breakfast, grabbed him, and dragged him back toward the gate of the property.

Tirin looked at the house, carefully eyeing each window for movement. Tirin sighed with relief as the curtains to every window remained still before turning to face Darec, who simply looked at her with a large grin.

"I'm sorry, did I startle you?" he asked, his voice trembling with laughter.

Tirin raised her pert little nose and looked away from him. "You will have to do more than that to scare me, Darec." She started to walk away and frowned as the Young Lord followed her.

"What're you up to?" he asked again, keeping her pace with ease.

"What makes you think that I'm up to something? Aren't you the Lord of mischief?" She picked up her pace a little and watched as he did too.

Darec shook his head and memories of the past filled her. She remembered how she had been so attracted to him. How she wished that his heart would change to adore her. But lingering hatred rose to replace past adoration and with this she added more speed to her pace. The hatred still surprised her because she couldn't remember why she felt that way. Yes, he used to bully her when they were younger, but he had changed as the years went on. Still, she was missing something, something horrible that he had done, and no matter what she did, she couldn't remember what it was.

Darec watched her pull away, smiling as she continued to act suspicious. He remembered how it had been between them before, too. He remembered clearly the abuse he and his friends put her through just because she was human. He couldn't understand why he wasn't trying to forget them or why he felt no remorse for them. He looked around at the cheerful street. Just about each corner on any street had a memory of abuse for Tirin. Darec looked up and found that she had more than doubled the distance between them. He rushed to catch up, picking random flowers as he did. He noticed how bothered she seemed at his persistence to keep up with her and smiled.

"What?" she asked annoyed. He smiled as he handed her the small bouquet of flowers. She tried to fight it, but found it hard not to smile. Her brown face reddened as she tried to keep her eyes on the flowers.

"What's this for?" She looked around to see if anyone had witnessed the gift. "You know what they would think if anyone saw this." He shrugged and she wished there was at least one person out there to see this. Tirin silently reprimanded herself for such a selfish thought. Daynel Amforle wouldn't be jealous of such a menial gift from the one that she had vowed would be her husband.

"Your thoughts are the only ones that matter." She looked at him. "But seriously now, Tirin. What are you up to?"

Tirin continued to look at him, a little confused.

"Tirin."

Tirin blinked her confusion away as she realized she was losing time. "I'm going on a trip."

Darec laughed. "Today's a Comne, you can't go anywhere." He grinned at her. "Your father would skin you if you left."

"My father's preoccupied," she said impatiently. "And I can go where I please. I'm not an elf."

The Young Lord looked at her, slightly amused. "No, but you are the daughter of a High Imperial guard... "

"Retired!" She cut him off, irritated.

Darec shook his head. "If a war was to suddenly come up, whom do you think my father would call upon? The new Imperial or the old?"

She looked away from him, saying nothing as she continued to walk.

"Tirin! Tirin, don't be angry. We all have to..." She whirled on him, her large brown eyes threatening tears.

"How would you feel in my place? Having to be forced to go to every Comne that could never be yours?" She swallowed the urge to cry, refusing to let him see that. Darec grabbed her arm and led her toward a more isolated area.

"I know what you're going through." He forced her to look into his eyes by gently turning her face to his, making her see that he sympathized with her. "Being who I am, I have to constantly go to meetings and other gatherings just because I'm my father's only heir."

Tirin shook her head and pulled away from him. "Not the same!" she hissed. "Not the same at all!"

She pointed back toward the street, indicating the excitement the people had and the decorations that would soon take over the whole area.

"My heart is filled with jealousy, Darec, because of what you and your friends in the past made me realize over and over again. I'm human, not an Ao'lean elf. I can never enjoy these Comnes because I..."

Darec's hand slid down the length of her arm to hold her hand, gently intertwining his fingers with hers. She looked at him, her tongue frozen.

"That's not the only reason for the Comne, Tirin," he said with a wistful gaze. "It's also to welcome young elves and in your case, a young human, into adulthood. It's a time for realizing that childish ways are now to be put away. It's time to think on your future, to prepare for marriage, make new families..."

Tirin's heart suddenly stopped. All this time she'd been looking a Comne the wrong way. She'd wanted to show all of Ao'lean that she did belong and then realized that her magyk could cause her to be banished or executed. It never occurred to her that the main reason for their excitement in this celebration was to see who got whom. She hadn't even considered that.

Her depression deepened; who would want a human for a wife? The life span of an elf could go on for several hundred years and they aged slowly while her kind, if lived carefully, could only last maybe a few years past a hundred. Daynel was going to have a ball on her behalf. What man would want a short relationship with a woman they knew would die long before they did? The idea of having children with her was ridiculous; what father would want to outlive their children due to her blood? Tirin jerked away from Darec and ran full tilt toward the main gates, quickly leaving him behind. He watched as she disappeared down the road.

Antoinette J. Houston

CHAPTER THREE

Kiss

The wind picked up, then quickly tapered off into a breeze. The scent of honey and caphony flowers surrounded him. Tyrus cocked his head, confused. What was Tirin doing in the forest? Today was a Comne and she knew to remain home. He breathed in the scent of her perfume deeply. It was thin, which meant that she was some distance from him, and he needed to change that quickly before she left the area.

It didn't take him long to locate her as her sobs led him straight to her. He approached her quietly as she sat at the base of a tree, curled up with her arms covering her head. He knelt down beside her and started to greet her.

With a shrill scream Tirin shoved him away and scrambled to her feet as she felt his breath on her arm. Tyrus bit his lip at the sudden urge to laugh as he moved quickly to intercept her when she took off blindly.

"Tirin!" He grabbed her by her shoulders and turned her around. "Tirin, it is I!" He couldn't control the smile that surfaced upon his face as she finally looked at him.

She sighed, resting her head against his chest and hugging him. His smile faltered as his breath caught in his throat. He could feel the frantic beat of her heart as she pressed him against her. Tirin

31

released him as she turned to look back toward Ao'lean. She didn't notice the strange look on his face. Tirin faced him again, her relief changing to mock anger as she punched him playfully in the stomach.

"What're you trying to do? Give me a heart attack?" Tirin turned and found another spot at the base of another tree. She looked at him, suddenly smiling, because what she thought was a trick of her mind was true. "Why, Tyrus. You're smiling!"

She watched him try to relax his face and the smile vanished, but then without warning, it reappeared.

"I cannot seem to help it." He shrugged when he moved to stand over her. "Why are you out here and what has Darec done now?"

Her grin faltered as the seriousness of today took over. "What he's always done." She sighed. "Opened his mouth when he shouldn't."

Tyrus looked at her, confused, and for a moment she lost her train of thought when his larger than normal violet eyes seem to swallow her.

"Are you going to explain what he said or is it a secret?"

She snapped out of his spell, not realizing that she had been staring. "Um…Well, he…he just made me realize what a fool I've been all this time." She frowned. "Trying to be accepted as one of you when no matter what gift I possess, it won't change what I am."

Tyrus saw her face cloud over and her mouth work soundlessly before she looked up from her fidgeting hands. "He … "

Without warning, she burst into tears again. Tyrus moved quickly, putting his arms around her and holding her. It took a moment for him to realize that he'd never touched her this way before, and she might find it strange that his usual icy character now had compassion. All he cared about was whatever Darec had said was causing her grief.

"What did he say, *Cattea*?" The word meant 'little bird' and she couldn't help but smile a little. Her father called her that often and she found it strange yet oddly comfortable that Tyrus used it as well. Her smile faded as she saw the look on his face. It was a look that promised some type of violent action, more than likely toward Darec.

She wiped her eyes, a halfhearted laugh escaping. "No, it's not really his fault that I'm crying. He was only stating the obvious, or what should've been." She wiped away the last of her tears. "I'm human and no matter what I do I will always be." She patted his face, watching warily until the protective look faded. "He just reminded me that the Comne wasn't just for showing off talents, but to see who was ..." She pouted as she lost her voice to emotion.

"What?" Tyrus whispered.

Tirin unfolded her legs and stretched them out very unlady-like. "To see who was attracted to whom." She looked at him pitifully.

Tyrus pulled back. "Oh. That." He looked away. "Forgive my ignorance."

"Ignorance is right." She looked at him.

He scratched his head and looked up at the sky. "Now I am in trouble with you."

She shook her head. "I'll never understand why you do what you do to yourself. Alienate yourself from everyone at every Comne. Even I don't do that. Even with your curse, you have something to look forward to in your future. Isn't there anyone you're attracted to?"

He turned away, his blithe disposition dimming. "Who would want a dog for a husband?" he stated quietly. "My curse is not the sole reason I have lost interest in the Comne, but because of the stupid pride of this place. They all only care about what someone else would think." He looked at her. "You, on the other hand, have a number of young men interested in you, even though human. You..."

"Have less of a chance than you do, apparently, as none of them are brave enough to make the attempt to ask. You still have the choice of taking a bride, if you could ever get over your selfishness." She looked at him, annoyed. "I can't convince anyone here to take a chance on me."

Tyrus simply looked at her.

"Tyrus, I'm human! What elf in their right mind would want to get into a relationship only to suffer heartache in a couple of decades?" She crossed her arms over her chest. "Even if someone was to show interest in me, could I dare to be selfish and see it through to marriage? Elves can live for several hundreds of years. humans can barely live over a hundred. I'm frail as it is, Tyrus, and when I'm sixty I will become only a burden to them as they will still be able to do things that a youth can do."

Tyrus shook his head. "You really should not think of it that way. You do not know what the future holds for you." He stood up from her. "Being that you have a talent and the Grand Ao'lean will recognize it even though you are human..."

Tirin looked at him in shock. She didn't remember saying anything about having magyk to him.

"You implied, I assumed," he said, seeing her worry.

She thought she was more guarded with her words. She fidgeted nervously; she didn't think she could take it if Tyrus turned against her. "Are...are you...?"

He knelt down beside her. "I am not afraid or sad, or any other negative emotion you could think of. I am happy for you." He stood back up and leaned against the tree, the sudden urge to caress her face strong. "This is why you are really running out on the Comne, is it not?"

She looked up at him. "They'll hate me, and I know it! There is no story they have that shows a human being sane with magyk.

They'll jump to the conclusion that I'll go mad and have me thrown out."

"Your father would not hear of it. Besides, Bayne is human. She is not crazy nor is she evil…"

"Have you forgotten that she cursed you?" Tirin frowned, confused.

He shrugged. "I brought that upon myself. She is in the swamps for privacy, I trespassed, and she punished me," he replied humbly.

They were silent for a while. Tirin wondered how she could go back when she could easily be banished. Tyrus just watched her fret. Though he knew it to be selfish, he wanted her to go back so he could watch the faces of all of those gathered. He wanted to see them realize that they were not as special as they thought. That the Barryn thought this wonderful human girl special, and allowed her the rights they took for granted.

"Have you told your father?"

She looked at him and laughed. "I didn't really give myself a chance to think this through."

They were silent again as she rounded up the courage to ask her next question.

"Tyrus?" She paused because she found her fingers were entangled in her skirt.

Tyrus smiled inwardly. "Yes?" He knew her question was going to be something that would embarrass her. She was probably going to ask the names of her other admirers. He knew of a few, but…

"Do you find me attractive?" she asked suddenly, her earthy complexion reddening a bit with a blush as she looked at him.

He blinked. He didn't know what to say. "I…" He swallowed; dare he tell her the truth? Was she asking in response to his uncharacteristic concern earlier or was she just inquiring? He couldn't lie to her either way. As he got ready to answer, she stood up.

Tirin watched, disappointed, as his face remained as stony as always beneath his wild midnight hair. She almost laughed aloud at herself for expecting more.

"Yes."

"Really?" She couldn't control the shock that filled her face. She watched him nod, becoming almost alarmed when his stony façade softened and his golden skin flushed. She was confused by this reaction. The only expression Tyrus ever made clear since his being cursed was one of annoyance with everyone. Now his eyes were full of something she didn't understand. She paused. What did this mean?

"As a full-blooded elf, do you think you could marry me?" she asked quietly. "Would you take me as a life mate?" Her stomach flipped and her heart did a strange rhythm in her chest as for the first time she saw Tyrus as more than just the caring friend and self-appointed bodyguard. She saw how handsome he was in his own dark way.

Tyrus realized that he was taking a chance. Could he tell her, would he tell her, that he loved her?

"Yes." He nodded again.

Tirin couldn't believe if this was the way Tyrus truly felt or was he just saying it to be nice?

Tirin swallowed hard but forced herself to continue this torture. "You could with your whole heart risk your heart to love me? Knowing that my years are far shorter than your own?" She tried to back away as he took her hand, fearing that he might be able to sense her sudden confusion. She became paranoid, thinking he could hear her heart pounding in her chest.

Tyrus took a breath of excitement as she looked nervously at him. He could hear her heart and it only excited him. Was she secretly in love with him as well? He was going for it. He was going to tell her, right here, right now.

"Tirin, I…"

"Should I be jealous?"

Both Tirin and Tyrus jumped at his voice. Darec raises a brow in curious surprise. "Well. I really would like to know what you two were talking about. Tyrus didn't even hear me…must've been a serious conversation."

Tirin watched, growing fearful of Tyrus' silence as he pulled away quickly. His irritation with Darec's timing hid his temporary lack of emotional restraint.

"What were you going to say, Tyrus?" Tirin asked almost pleadingly. Tyrus looked at her and then at Darec.

"Sire Baelor will be very upset if you do not return home." Tyrus watched her face fall, saw her disappointment slowly turn into swelling anger. He felt ashamed as she glared at him.

"Coward," she whispered heatedly, low enough that only he with his wolf-like hearing could hear. His eyes dropped to the ground.

"What was that?" Darec asked.

Tirin looked at him. "Go away, both of you!" She turned and stormed off. Tyrus started after her only to be stopped by Darec.

"I'll handle it; you've seemed to have annoyed her somehow." Darec smiled.

Tyrus watched quietly as Darec chased after her. Why had he become suddenly bashful when Darec showed up?

Tirin continued to walk then stopped and whirled about as she heard footsteps. Hoping it was Tyrus coming to apologize, she was surprised to see Darec standing there.

"Go away!" she snapped.

Darec continued to walk up to her, stopping only when he was toe to toe with her. He smiled as she stood her ground and refused to back up.

"I have always loved your stubbornness."

Tirin looked at him suspiciously. "What?"

He took her hand and grinned. "May I escort you to the Comne?" He released her hand and wrapped his arms about her waist, drawing her closer. "May I be your *intaidea*?" he asked quietly as he nuzzled her neck boldly. He grinned wider as he felt her body stiffen, but she was too shocked to do anything about it.

"My...my, my intended? But, what...I mean--" She swallowed hard as she gently freed herself from him. He watched, amused, as her wide eyes suddenly narrowed. "I don't want your pity, Darec," she snapped after seeing his grin.

"What pity?" he said, genuinely confused. "I'm being brutally honest to you about how I feel. Tirin, I want to be with you. Have wanted to be with you for a while now. There's no pity in the way I feel."

She looked at him. "One of your jokes, I know it. You know that no one else would dare ask to escort me so you make the ultimate sacrifice and..."

"You really don't pay much attention to the people you try so hard to impress, do you?" Darec watched her face take on a look of childish defiance. "If you had, you would know, probably hear, the talk of who's going to ask Tirin to the Comne? Why do you think I got up so early to greet you this morning?" He crossed his arms. "I don't get up that early for breakfast."

She mimicked his defensive posture, not sure what was going on as Darec continued. "I'm not the only one, just the smartest." He moved to take her hand again. "I figured that if I didn't make my move as early as possible I would lose out to either Josam or Miread."

"Josam?" She gave him a suspicious look. "You wouldn't lie to me, would you?" She watched as he shook his head. "Then the answer to your question is 'No.'"

Darec's mouth dropped. "No?"

Tirin nodded. "No."

He laughed a little. "Why not? I don't understand."

Tirin smiled. "All this time I've been worried about not impressing anyone and you and Tyrus have both proved me wrong." She twirled about. "I want to meet these so-called suitors you both claim I have."

He relaxed a little, relieved to know what she and Tyrus were talking about. "So you don't believe us."

"That, and besides, what fun would it be if I just took the first offer without even considering others?" She watched his face carefully, feeling shamefully pleased when his arrogant grin melted away.

"But it's not…"

"Fair?" Tirin gave him cold look. "My whole life was unfair." The feeling of shame grew in her chest, forcing her freezing heart to warm up. She sighed. "Darec, honestly, I'm more than flattered that you have offered to escort me, but now that I know you are not the only one…do you know how long I've waited…dreamed of having admirers? Being human and all? You think I want to close the door on something as exciting as this?"

Darec was smiling but she could see it was hollow. He stood frozen, unsure what to do next, as he had never been turned down before. Tirin chewed her lip thoughtfully. "Darec, forgive my selfishness. I want to meet all…" She started to move closer at the same time he did. Wrapping his arms about her again, bringing her face to his, he kissed her. She froze in shock, unable to understand why she was doing nothing. The kiss ended and she gawked at him for a moment. Her face was practically on fire from the sudden rush of blood. She gave off a strangled squeak before she took off running, heading back home.

He followed at a casual walk, soon running into Tyrus, who had remained where they had left him. He stood there with his usual look of indifference. Darec rolled his eyes. "She's heading home. That's what you wanted, isn't it?"

Tyrus growled at him. "But what did you do? Why did she seem upset?"

Darec waved his words away. "I have no time to explain myself to you. If you must know, she's not upset, just…excited. I informed her of a few who were taken with her." Tyrus watched as the Young Lord continued back toward Ao'lean, knowing that there was more to the story than Darec was letting on.

Tirin ran blindly. Why had she let him get away with that? If her father ever found out…had Tyrus seen? She saw the moment over a hundred times in her head as she ran. She couldn't possibly want him romantically now…could she?

The sound of her boots on stone brought her back to reality as she ran through the square. She came to an abrupt halt less than two hundred yards from the front gate of her home. The urge to scream was so strong! How could that little kiss, one that didn't even mean anything, turn her around? She looked at the windows and saw her father standing in one, watching her. She sighed and the distance between her and home shrank.

Baelor Desgjin watched his daughter walk solemnly into the garden, slowly making her way toward the house. How she looked just like her mother! Sire Baelor remembered how hateful he'd felt toward all humans those many years ago. How the memory of his capture and the torture he and those under his command suffered, not only in pain but also in humiliation, by those who had caught them. How they had suffered ultimate humiliation when their barbaric captors amputated their sword arms. Infection killed off a few, and suicide was the answer for some to their captors' promise of slavery. Save him. It was not that he wanted to return to his new wife back in Ao'lean. Nor was it that he was too proud. It was the plain fact that he didn't want to die.

He had been enslaved for two years to 'Master' Borod before meeting Zola, Tirin's mother. They had met in the market. He had been sent on the morning errands, a show of 'Master' Barod's prized Imperial Captain turned lowly slave. She had run into him trying to escape from some drunken ruffians. His hatred had turned into indifference and he didn't care about anything, not even himself. She used him as a shield, telling her attackers some made-up berserk story about him. It worked even though he simply stood there, his arms full of produce. Reluctantly they became friends after that day. He remembered how Zola used to tease him, how she always knew what to say to make him feel better. He sighed. How he missed Zola.

Baelor snapped out of the memory as the front door slammed shut. He shrugged off the melancholy emotions and headed out to greet his adopted daughter. Tirin watched him move from the library to the top of the stairs. She planted her hands on her hips and stared up at him.

"I'm not going." She remained silent as her father groaned. She watched him take another deep breath before rolling his eyes. He'd known she would pull something today. He was surprised that she even returned home.

"Don't start, *Cattea*," he warned.

"Why, Father? Why do I have to suffer like this?" she asked pitifully.

"Stop being childish, Tirin. You're going." He started down the stairs toward her. "You know the procedure. You know what's required of you."

She pouted, crossing her arms in disgust. "I... may," she started, then stopped. "No." She shook her head. "I'm not going."

"You started to change your mind," he said suspiciously. "What was that about?"

"Darec and Tyrus claim there are some young men who have romantic interests in me. Despite my outward appearance."

He smiled. "And that surprises you?"

She started to grin shyly, then stomped her foot. "No! It doesn't matter. My not being an elf means…"

"You say any disparaging word concerning yourself and I will spank you," Baelor said sternly as he reached the bottom of the stairs.

She glared at him. "I can't believe you!" she snapped. "What does it matter if I go or not? It's not like anyone will miss me!" She ran past him up the stairs.

He groaned as she slammed the door to her room. "Start getting dressed!" he yelled.

"So she came home," Tyrus said behind him.

Baelor turned to face the younger elf, startled, as the boy had made no noise. He had often wondered about Tyrus' predicament. He saw the changes in his appearance despite his efforts to hide them with his unruly black hair.

"So I have you to thank for her return?" Baelor's earlier smile broadened and he watched, confused, as Tyrus shook his head.

"Thank the Young Lord." He quietly moved up the stairs toward his own room.

"Darec, again." Baelor sighed as he headed into the den. He went to the thick velvet curtains that shut out the afternoon sun and quickly pulled one panel back. "One day, Tyrus, whatever is bothering you about your once closest friend will surface." He looked out the window. "And I probably won't like it." He moved toward the nearest shelf. The sunlight illuminated the dust motes that floated through the room, giving it an ancient feel. The old duskwood shelf groaned low as he pressed his shoulder against the books that filled the fourth shelf. He blindly reached behind the old books, his fingers feeling along the back of the shelving for the small hidden cache.

Baelor smiled as his fingers brushed the worn wood of the small container. He pulled it out into the sunlight, revealing a dust-covered jewelry box. Its contents softly knocked about inside. He opened it and couldn't help but smile. Zola would have wanted her to have this on an occasion such as this. He paused. Had she lived, he wondered where he would be and what life would have held for him. He often wondered what had brought her back to him that fateful night, and why whoever Tirin's father was didn't escort her...

Baelor lowered the lid of the jewelry box and took a deep breath.

Tirin considered her reflection in the mirror that had once belonged to her stepmother. The stepmother she'd never met. Loa Desgjin had died two years before Tirin's birth and from her father's reactions Loa would not have cared to know of Tirin. That was the reaction she was afraid of. It didn't matter what Darec or Tyrus said to ease her nervousness; she knew there would be some who would look at her as if she was a daemon. She could still run off without her father's knowing. Be the coward she so wanted to be. Risk her father going mad with both humiliation and hellish anger.

Tirin closed her eyes and sighed.

She looked at herself in the mirror again, this time trying to be positive. It was the first time in a long time she had dressed this well. She turned to get a better look at herself; this attire made her look more her age. She could probably get a reaction out of Tyrus with this dress. She grinned at herself, surprised at that thought. Exactly how much did she care for him? Was it more than just amiable and why did these feelings appear now, at a time that would prove to be the most trying? Her stomach quivered with a strange fluttery feeling as she recalled Tyrus' eyes. How he'd looked at her. Did he really care for her? Had he been talking about how *he* truly felt or was he simply giving insight on what *could* happen? She pressed her hands against her stomach thinking she would feel it. The sensation vanished. She exhaled softly and looked at her appearance again in the old mirror.

Tirin tilted her head to the side and smiled at the idea that she had admirers, people who were actually taken with her! The thought that Darec...she paused, reflecting on what happened in the forest.

Darec himself was taken with her. What was she to do about him? She had to admit that she found it appealing that he wanted her, but she didn't want to want him. Romantic feelings such as this she thought she left behind long ago. She couldn't possibly feel that way about him now. She knew he had done something to her, something terrible, but she couldn't remember what. Her inability to react appropriately to his advance scared her as well. She sat down upon the corner of her bed and put on her dress boots. She was so confused. She wanted to run away yet she wanted to stay, curious to see who would dare approach her. She sighed; her life was going to change drastically, either for the good or bad. She might impress the young males here enough to warrant their admiration, or she might be banished from the only place she had ever called home because of a gift of magykal ability. Should she stay or should she leave?

A soft knock on the door jarred her from her thoughts. For a moment, she simply stared at the handle, then she answered. "Come in."

Slowly the door opened and her father stepped in. He looked younger in his uniform with all his medals and honors. Still, she remained impassive, refusing to give him any sign of approval. Baelor looked at her, at first a little wary, and then smiling as he entered the room. "You look beautiful, *Cattea*."

"That doesn't change my mood," she said quietly.

Baelor moved to sit beside her. "Regardless of your mood, Tirin, it gives you no right to ignore your obligations."

"How is it my obligation?" She stood up from him.

He gave her a stern look and she sat back down. "I'm not going to have any fun."

He touched her face. "You have not the slightest idea what this evening holds for you." He watched her give a small nervous laugh. "Tirin, what is it?"

"Nothing…" she trailed off.

"Well since it's nothing then let's move on." He reached into his pocket and removed the small box. "Here."

She looked at the box then at him. "What is…?"

He pushed the box toward her. "I hold the box for you to open. Look."

She sat still for a moment, then sighed and took the box. It was old, whatever it was. Its container was worn, the formerly smooth wood covering weather-beaten and cracked, what her father would have described as personality. She lifted the lid and something sparkled brightly from its deep hollow. Small stones embedded in a web of fine silver made up a delicate necklace. As she gazed in awe, her attention was drawn to the stones rather than the craftsmanship. The stones she knew all by heart: the bright yellow flaym, the deep bloodstone, a glistening waterbead, the clear star rock, a pitch nightstone. These were oddly brighter than the others, like they had an inner fire. She looked at her father as she lifted the necklace free of its case. A strange tingling traced a line from the ornament down her arm.

"It's magykal?" she asked as the feeling faded. The stones ranged in size and there were six more which were strangely muted. Baelor took the necklace and urged her toward the mirror.

"I have to see you put it on. The necklace is what your mother called a spell catcher."

She stared at her reflection in the mirror as she opened the latch of the adornment and fastened it around her neck. "My…mother?" she whispered.

"Watch." He pointed to the necklace's reflection. "It's supposed to protect the wearer as well as catch spells for the wearer to use. The plus to it is that no one can remove it from your neck except you."

Tirin's eyes widened as the stones seemed to rearrange themselves in the web, growing brighter before becoming still. Now the earth's pearl and the cat's eye were just as bright as the other five. Baelor cocked his head.

"You've been practicing on your own, huh?" He smiled at her knowingly. "You've added two more spells." She stared at him.

"What does that mean?"

He shrugged. "Honestly I don't know how it works, but your mother said that it took her twelve years to fill up the first five and you've filled two within seconds."

She looked in the mirror at the necklace again. "That still doesn't tell me what it does."

"That is a mystery you will have to solve on your own."

Tyrus watched, unnoticed, from the doorway as Tirin and Sire Baelor discussed her inheritance. He knew how she felt, wishing with all his heart that he had been a better son to his own mother. He could see how Baelor missed Tirin's mother almost as much as she did. Their relationship had been more than just friendly, he figured. He could see the hurt in both of them as they spoke quietly over the necklace, see how Tirin wished she could have met her, and how Sire Baelor wished she had lived.

Tyrus couldn't help but wonder if Tirin's mother had lived, would Baelor have brought her here or taken off for other territories? Was Tirin the product of a forbidden love affair or was she truly someone else's child? He tied his hair back as he calmed his restless thoughts. These things were not for him to worry about.

Tyrus watched Tirin smile as she touched the necklace. He held his breath as she unconsciously caressed her neck and shoulders while admiring the way the necklace looked on her. She seemed at ease for the moment, but he knew what the night held in store for her. How worried she had been in the woods and how worried he was for her. He sighed, knowing that her fears could actually come true. Even though Tirin was as much a part of Ao'lean as the rest of them, he knew firsthand of their paranoia. He knew how they treated anyone different from them. His curse was the only thing that made him different and that was more than enough to warrant being shunned. The idea of her being banished was not farfetched. If her being accepted was seen as a bad omen of some sort, they could, and more than likely would, banish her. Despite her father's arguments and the High Lord's actions, the people of Ao'lean would see her exiled. He swallowed. There would be no doubt in his leaving along with Baelor and Tirin if it was to happen.

Tyrus brushed loose strands of hair from his face when the fact of the matter finally hit him. How selfish of him to want her to go through with the whole ritual, to see the Comne and the Barryn through to the end. To watch her suffer the stares and the unnecessary pity from those who never gave her the chance to show them how wonderful she was. Just to see the looks on this town's collective faces when a human was granted a gift. He wanted her to be accepted by a tree of great wisdom when its people refused to. He wanted to revel in their surprise and guilt when the greatest of them all could do nothing to prevent the Grand Ao'lean from seeing her worthy enough to be granted a rite only they had received in the past.

Tyrus watched Tirin turn away from her father for a moment, hiding her brief frown. He could sense her confusion, could feel it as if it were his own. How unsure she was. Then it came to him. He leaned on the low table just outside her room in an attempt to keep her in sight as she moved from one area to another. He could escort her to Wonderlost, provided she showed him what kept her out at night.

The table slipped beneath his weight, giving off a loud noise.

Tirin looked away from her reflection to the door then moved quickly to see who was there.

Baelor watched while she searched the hallway. Was there interest between his daughter and Tyrus? He smiled. He knew of Tyrus' feeling for her even with the boy's refusal to express himself. The way he carried himself around her spoke loud enough.

"What are you looking for, Tirin? Who else could it be?" He stood up from the bed. Maybe he should interfere for the boy and let Tirin know of his feelings.

Tirin turned to see her father in deep thought and grew slightly concerned when his hand came up to stroke his beard.

"What is it?"

Baelor grinned, then shook his head. "Nothing, Cattea."

"I wanted us to go together." She moved toward the window and watched Tyrus quickly moving through the garden, pausing to look briefly up at her window before moving on. She sighed when Baelor walked over and hugged her.

"Don't worry, he'll be there." He wouldn't meddle in such a delicate matter; he respected the boy too much. If he wanted Tirin to know of his feelings, he would tell her in his own time. Baelor sighed. Hopefully it would be soon.

Tirin gave a loud and pitiful sigh before dropping her hands to her sides.

"Okay, let's get this drudgery over with."

Baelor rolled his eyes before he motioned for her hand.

CHAPTER FOUR

Magyk

Tyrus moved quickly beyond the garden, looking up at Tirin's window to meet her gaze before moving on. He couldn't help but feel there was something there. Maybe there was a chance at love for the two of them. He felt as if he had his own personal sun all of a sudden. The thought that she could be as taken with him as he was with her was more than pleasing. His sunshine turned to gray clouds as reality set in. Would she really take him? His becoming a wolf often could prove a problem.

The cursed wolf and the mad witch. He couldn't help but scoff. He covered his face; there was no way she would take him for a husband! The majority of their relationship would find him on all fours! He needed to stop being such a coward and confront the old witch and soon before someone else saw Tirin for more than just human. He moaned and continued to walk blindly. Tonight would prove most trying as he knew of a few who were going to make their attempts for her heart. Especially Darec. He growled softly before stopping suddenly in front of a house.

It was a foul, rotting odor that had caused him to pause. Tyrus looked around, finding himself in front of what used to be his home. He found himself suddenly cold as memories from six years ago came rushing back.

After failing his dare earlier that day, Tyrus had to deal with being called a coward for the rest of the day. The taunts that Darec and his other friends threw at him were no comparison to the threat from the witch for attempting to steal her staff. Her threat seemed to echo and follow him all day. Her hate-filled words wrapped around him tightly even through his Barryn ritual. His Barryn had been odd to begin with: he was only sixteen when the Grand Ao'lean had called him. He found himself unable to be good company when he came out with the others when it ended. He had been given a vision of a large, white wolf daemon holding the body of a girl...one who looked like Tirin. That was all he received from the great tree. Even as disturbing as that was, his mind was more concerned with the witch's threat. His bed promised him a fretful sleep filled with nightmares.

Tyrus awoke with a start later that night. His heart pounded in his ears as pieces of his nightmare flashed in his mind. He went to wipe his face only to find to his horror that his nightmare was reality! He howled in dismay, for his elven body had been transformed within the dream into a monstrous wolf! Clumsily he fell to the floor with a thud, the entangled covers falling on top of him. He froze as the footsteps of his mother grew louder, then his door opened and she entered. Her soft laughter at the heap on the floor echoed eerily through his room.

"Was the dream that bad, dirdie?" she asked as she walked over to help him.

He tried to warn her, tried to tell her to just go away, only to hear himself growl.

"Did you just growl at me? How rude!" She continued to unwrap the sheets, a smile still on her face. "A mother is allowed to help her little dirdie when he need...oh."

Childish anger flashed through him; he had always had a problem getting his mother to leave him be when he wanted to be left alone. She was always spouting that mother's duty decree.

'I told you to leave me...' he tried to say, but her look as she backed away reminded him of his predicament. His angry growls echoed in his ears.

"Oh...Oh my..." She was gasping for air. Her right hand grabbed at her chest as she fell to the floor. She was having a heart attack!

Tyrus freed himself of his blankets and ran for the stairs, his only thought that his mother was dying. In his urgency, he forgot his own dilemma even when he was unable to grasp the doorknob. He found an open window and used it as an escape.

It was close to sunrise as the birds were chirping and the lamps were being extinguished. His claws resounded loudly off the cobblestone lanes as he followed their winding routes, desperately searching for anyone to help. As he came over the hill of the next street, he found a group of them. A handful of High guards were assisting the lamp man with his chore. Tyrus called to them, at first confused as they all jumped, two of them drawing their swords. He then remembered why, but it was a little too late as one of them pointed at him. Tyrus skidded to a halt as they turned to face him. No one moved at first. The guards just stared in obvious surprise at the monstrous black wolf that seemed to have found its way into the city. Tyrus knew that with his size the thought in their mind was not to just capture him. He posed a threat to the city. He looked at the guards again and almost wet himself as two of them were gone! He looked about and saw that they had somehow circled around him.

"The monster's not a normal dog, he knows what you're doing," the lamp man said from his ladder.

"Hush, Gaeril!" hissed the nearest guard.

Tyrus cowered at the sound of their gloved hands tightening on the leatherbound hilts. He couldn't help his mother if he was dead.

"Please!" he barked, quickly reprimanding himself for forgetting. He took off with the guards yelling behind him as he darted between them and headed toward the palace. Darec could help him, at least he hoped he could. He heard the footsteps of the guards behind him and the lamp man yelling to wake the people, warning of a monster loose on the street.

There was no help, this was no dream, and by now his mother was dead. He howled miserably as he ducked and dodged through bushes and fences. He didn't know where to go or who would help him. How could anyone help him? They wouldn't know he was an elf.

He slammed into a guard coming from the opposite direction, sending both of them sprawling. The collision redirected his frantic run. By now the main gates were closed; there was no escape now. He loped up the street, his eyes looking frantically for relief. They landed on what he thought at first a ghost. Tyrus ran toward her, not thinking how strange it was for Tirin to be standing out on the street in her nightgown. As he neared her, he half expected her to run into the house screaming, but instead, to his surprise, she moved to the side, letting him in. Tyrus did not slow; he continued to run up the path to the front door. It opened, as Baelor was on his way out to call Tirin back in when Tyrus bolted past.

"What in the..." Baelor yelled as he was forced back against the wall. He ran to retrieve his weapon only to meet Tirin in the hallway. She held him back.

"Don't be hasty, Father." Tirin watched as Tyrus scrambled up the stairs. "He's no danger. Bar them from entering, please?" she asked calmly, pointing to the front door.

Baelor watched his daughter follow the wolf. He was confused but strangely calmed by the fact that she didn't seem affected at all by the urgency of the situation. He barred the door.

"Baelor! What are you doing, man?" one of the residents yelled.

Baelor shrugged as he looked back toward the stairs.

"If you truly care for that..." another started, falling silent as Baelor turned sharply, a threatening look on his face as he leveled his sword with the speaker's throat.

"Were you really going to finish that statement, Lorel?"

There was a thud and a series of whimpers from upstairs, grabbing Baelor's attention again.

"You may bring them up, Father!" Tirin called down. Still confused, Baelor obeyed his daughter's request and led the overly excited crowd up to her bedroom.

"Tirin, I hope you know what you're getting yourself into, girl," he said as he entered first.

"Listen to your father, Tirin!" one of the guards warned. "Get away from the beast and let us handle it."

"Allow you to murder one of your own?" Tirin said as she stood in front of the beast. "I couldn't let that happen."

Both Tyrus and Baelor looked at her in surprise.

"Tirin, what are you talking about? One of us?" her father asked.

Tirin knelt in front of Tyrus, not at all afraid. "There is no one else I know who has eyes like these. Not a normal animal this," she said in an odd tone.

Baelor glared at the crowd behind him, silently ordering them to stay put as he moved to see what she was seeing.

The wolf's large violet eyes stared back. "Oh, dear Goddess of all that's great! Is that Tyrus?"

The crowd hushed as she nodded. She got up from the floor and grabbed the sheet that was on her bed and draped it over the wolf.

"Tyrus, calm down."

Tyrus looked at her, then at her father, and then at the crowd. "Calm down? There is a mob of people behind you that would rather skin me than help me and you want me to calm...?" Tyrus knew his words were nothing but a series of growls and barks but he couldn't help himself.

Tirin looked at him and smiled secretly. "Yes. If you want me to help you're going to have to calm down."

Tyrus' jaw dropped. She understood him!

She almost laughed, seeming to sense his surprise. "Due to you and your friends, I have a lot of time to myself." She watched as he bowed his head shamefully.

Tirin put her hands on either side of his face, closed her eyes, and began whispering something in words he would never understand. Warmth spread from her hands to enfold his head and then body. Slowly this comforting warmth stretched throughout him, making it hard for him not to relax. His forepaws were the first sign, and he watched half-aware as they began to elongate. The long fur shrank back into his skin slowly at first, then gradually quickening as it worked its way over his body.

Tyrus looked at Tirin, who just looked tiredly back at him.

"Thank you," he whispered. "Thank you for saving my life, Tirin!" he yelled as he hugged her tightly, begging her forgiveness and pledging his loyalty to her all in one breath.

Tyrus looked back toward the Degjins' estate. Baelor had had a lot of explaining to do that night. The guards had tried to take Tirin when she forced him to revert. They had all known that her mother had been a blight-witch, but none of them had known that she had mystical abilities. Her alienation had doubled because of him that night.

They arrived at the Comne, Baelor watching his daughter fret silently all the way there. He wanted to urge her to either relax or to tell him about it, but felt that in her own time she would tell him.

The celebration was already underway, the Barryn ritual not far in starting. He smiled as the silversmiths' son, Kalin DaeLord, approached quietly and nervously from behind.

Tirin felt a gentle tug on her sleeve and turned to see a face she hadn't been expecting. He bowed deeply before taking her hand and a nervous breath.

"You are so beautiful." He blushed deeply then coughed, clearing his throat as he hadn't meant to say that. "I'm sorry...I meant, would you care to dance?"

Tirin was elated. Her worry faded drastically as her father smiled and pushed her to answer.

"Kalin, there was no need to apologize for your earlier remark." She smiled. "That just made my answer a positive one." She watched as his pasty face regained some of its color. "But."

His smile faltered.

"Is this of your own accord or did someone put you up to this?" She observed him closely, ignoring the sour look her father gave her.

Kalin swallowed hard and nodded. "I understand and no, this is not some childish prank, Tirin. I know I should have come and apologized for all the earlier trouble but..." He scratched his mousy brown head. "I...believe me, I'm ashamed of what I have done and would like for your forgiveness." He bowed again.

Tirin patted his shoulder before she bent down next to him. "It's all right. I forgave you when you said I was beautiful."

He grinned broadly. "And you are." He took her hand. "Shall we dance?"

Baelor watched as she smiled at him before being led away to the dance area. The young elf's friends greeted Tirin without incident and without bias and then music began.

He felt a large weight taken from his shoulders as she seemed to genuinely enjoy herself. For a good length of time he watched her go from dancing to just conversing with those she thought still hated her.

Baelor walked around the banquet table and grinned as he found his favorite dish.

"Baelor!"

The old elf jumped, dropping the Burgundy Mash and splattering the table with some of its syrupy wine-colored sauce. He turned to face the owner of the voice.

High Lord Deimiyon Shiey watched him with a grin that stretched from ear to ear. "So you got her to dance with someone after all these years only so you could get..."

"Why in all that's great did you do that?" Baelor snapped, annoyed. "I thought you were Tirin."

"I know." The High Lord laughed.

Baelor snatched the plate back up. "I deserve some reward every now and then."

Deimiyon grinned. "I suppose, but alas, my dear friend, you may not want to eat that just yet."

Baelor looked at his longtime friend. "What's with this tone? You're beginning to worry me."

"As it should." Deimiyon nodded. "I have news that concerns you and your daughter."

Baelor replaced the plate and waited. "Well? What is it?"

The High Lord took his friend by the arm and guided him away toward the grand Garden behind the Grand Ao'lean.

"You're worrying me, Deimiyon." Baelor stumbled twice as the High Lord dragged him from the party. "What is it?"

Deimiyon looked around as they reached the center of the Garden, making sure they were alone.

"What about Tirin, Deimiyon, what are you trying to do? Scare me to death? Tell me!"

Deimiyon sighed and pointed to a bench. "You should sit down."

"Don't start with me," Baelor warned. "Spit it out already!"

"Exactly how did you get Tirin?" he asked.

His friend rolled his eyes, annoyed. "Deimiyon!"

"All right, all right!" Deimiyon said, trying to calm him. "Your daughter's been called upon."

Baelor shook his head, cutting off his friend before he could finish.

"What you say is impossible, Deimiyon. Only an elf of Ao'lean can receive a gift, everyone knows that, even she knows that."

Deimiyon put his hands on Baelor's shoulders, forcing him to sit as he continued.

"I know this, but that doesn't change the fact that she's been called."

They were quiet for a moment, unaware that they now had an audience of one. Darec sat still in his hiding place, watching everything with full attention.

"I don't understand…how could this be?" Baelor asked, bewildered. "The only way this could be is if she was actually my daughter, by blood…but she isn't, not unless…" Baelor's eyes widened with renewed shock.

"Baelor, was there something you didn't mention? Like a relationship with this Zola?" Deimiyon said with a hint of disbelief.

Baelor covered his face, trying to remember. Twenty years earlier found him back in the town of Meadon. The town was going up in flames and he had just emerged from his cell for the past three years. A spell called the Watergate turned stone walls into what appeared to be standing water. As he walked through, he found Zola crumpled on the ground not far from his shelter, her blood coloring the ground as he neared her. In her weakening arms, she held a struggling bundle, Tirin. She was not even a year old and healthy, but soon to be motherless. Baelor carried the both of them beyond the boundaries of the burning town. Zola urged him to put her down, protesting that she wasn't going to make it no matter how hard he tried. As he set her down, she tried to explain with her last breath about Tirin. All she could get out was: "Tirin…Please forgive me."

All of this time he had thought she was telling him the child's name and asking for his forgiveness for leaving him and returning with another's baby.

Deimiyon nudged Baelor, as he seemed lost in memory. "Well? Did you have a relationship with this woman?"

"Yes."

"Were you intimate?"

"Yes."

Deimiyon closed his eyes in disbelief. "Is Tirin yours?"

Baelor yelled as he shot out of his seat. He couldn't believe himself! How could he not have seen it? The girl was so much like him! It wasn't because she was around him or because he raised her that way, but because she was his!

"I can't believe this is happening to me!" he growled. "How could I not see it?"

"So she is yours," Deimiyon said, sighing.

"Tirin is my daughter! She's got my blood coursing through her veins, so yes, she would be called." He struck the heel of his hand against his forehead. "Zola, oh Zola! Why couldn't you have lived?" He paused, looking through Deimiyon. "You would have lived longer if you hadn't come for me," he yelled angrily as he whirled about.

Deimiyon grabbed his arm. "Baelor, we don't have time for your guilt trip!"

Darec watched as Sire Baelor looked resignedly at the stars. Tirin was half elf! This would be something to tell. He thought about it; maybe it was news that should be discussed between daughter and father. Darec shook his head and grinned. He couldn't do it. He wanted to see the look on her face when he brought her the news. He knew it could be the whole night before Sire Baelor finally got the guts to tell his daughter that her adoptive father was actually her biological father. He found himself grinning all of a sudden. The women in Sire Baelor's family all had strong gifts, so Tirin was bound to receive the same level of ability. With her mother being a witch, her talent for magyk was bound to make her an important asset to the community. With his background and her magyk…Darec almost laughed aloud.

"You need to tell her as soon as possible," Deimiyon informed Baelor. He watched as Baelor paced back and forth, his fingers stroking his beard.

"Baelor…"

"I heard you!" Baelor snapped. "How? How do you tell your own daughter that you were so blind with jealousy that you didn't even realize that she was your own blood-related child?" He looked at Deimiyon with a questioning gaze. "That all her worries and most of what she's gone through could have been lessened or avoided in the first place?"

"Baelor…"

Baelor waved him quiet. "I need to be alone, Deimiyon. Please." Baelor walked deeper into the garden.

For weeks Zola had gone to see Baelor in secret, bringing him gifts of food, clothing, and her company. He eventually fell in love with her and for a while thought himself an idiot for doing so. He was an elf and a slave, what kind of a life could he give her? If she wanted him at all? As time passed, his feelings for her grew no

matter how he tried to resist. Often he ridiculed himself,
remembering how much he had hated humans before ever knowing
one.

One night she visited and seemed to be in a strange mood,
asking questions that he never thought she would ever be concerned
about. For long drawn-out moments there would be silence,
uncomfortable silence while she pondered his answers. Then, when
she was getting ready to leave, she came over and kissed him. He
was so startled he stood there, frozen, until she finished. She pulled
away when she received no immediate reaction. He tried to catch
her before she bolted, angry with himself for not reacting like he
wanted. But he was finally able to see how it Zola came and went as
she pleased without worry of being caught. Usually she left when he
was asleep or not paying attention.

She waved her hand in front of a wall, whispering what he
assumed to be a goodbye, and simply walked through it. He stood
there for a second then warily inspected the wall. It remained solid
for him.

He leaned against it, his heart heavy now. What had he
done? He slid to the floor, answers and questions filling his head.
Why hadn't he kissed her back? She ran because he didn't react. He
just stood there like a stone, unmoving. Was she a witch, a sorceress,
or a ghost? If she was a ghost, why him? If she was witch or
sorceress then why didn't she offer to help him escape? He put his
hand on the wall and stared at it for a moment. Would she come
back?

For days, she stayed away. She avoided him in town when he
was doing his master's business. With each day that passed he
worried that she had left, getting farther and farther away from this
town and from him. He had ruined a relationship that hadn't even
started.

Then one day, after being abused for slacking in his work,
she appeared again. Zola materialized through the west wall of his

small shack and this time he moved without realizing what he was doing. He walked over to her, watching as her eyes widened with either surprise at his motion or fright at his speed. He grabbed her and kissed her deeply. He finished the kiss and threatened to unite her body with his.

"I'm sorry." He nuzzled her neck, caressing her face with his. "I was just so surprised, I didn't think you would want..."

Zola looked at him, tears in her eyes as she smiled. "Because you're one arm short? Because you're a slave or an elf?" She hugged him back, watching his face. "I thought it was me. Because I was human and until recently I didn't think you'd give me a second chance after I revealed my little secret to you. I thought that maybe coupled with the fact that you're married already..."

His face did fall then. He held up his left wrist showing his Ao'lean band. He and Loa were joined by this band made from the wood of an Ao'lean tree and magykally solidified blood from both Loa and himself. Zola stared: instead of a vibrant crimson, it had changed to a dismal black color. He slammed his wrist against the nearest wall and the band shattered like glass.

"Baelor!"

He hushed her. "She's been dead for the past two years."

She touched his shoulder. "But you said nothing!"

He turned to her. "There was nothing to say. She had been sick for quite some time and I was in no shape to get to her." He turned away from her. "Besides, she wouldn't have me back. My people are extremely prideful; my lost arm would have embarrassed her. The fact that I've been enslaved for all these years by humans would have shamed me alone." He sighed. "This is the reason why most of my unit committed suicide. Why I never tried to escape. Where would I go? Who would I be of use to?"

Zola hugged him from behind. "You still have use." She smiled, turning him around.

Baelor could only grin.

Antoinette J. Houston

For the next few days they acted like love-starved fools, keeping their secret during the day and welcoming each other at night as if they would never see each other again.

One night as they laid in bed together, Baelor found himself wondering why she never offered to free him. Why she never wanted to talk about her own past or use whatever magyk she had to help them out of this town.

Zola watched his face grow serious while he unconsciously intertwined her fingers with his.

"What are you thinking about?"

He looked at her. "You."

She hugged him tight. "What about me?"

"Exactly what kind of witch or sorceress are you?"

He watched her composure change to defensiveness at his tone. "I find nothing wrong with either; I'm just confused as to why..."

"I never offered to help set you free?" She sat up, wrapping the covered about her. "That was my plan in the beginning, but then I fell in love with you and...I don't know."

Baelor took a breath and looked at her, a little perturbed, before he got out of bed.

"What kind of an excuse is that, Zola?"

She looked at him, her brown eyes large and shiny with coming tears. "I killed my mother."

He balked. "What?"

Her hands made weak attempts to tame her wild hair as he stared at her. "I haven't used my magyk in almost nine years. I had no reason to." She wiped her face. "I'm sorry for being selfish. I'm sorry for letting this go on like it has. I should've explained it to you long time ago."

"What are you babbling on about?" he asked, growing irritated. "I just want a simple answer as to why you haven't offered. To let us start a life together somewhere far from here."

Her eyes narrowed at his impatience. "Magyk has brought me nothing but trouble. Every time I used it something bad would happen. The last time I used it, I ended up having to run for my life."

He walked to the table and poured himself some of the wine she had brought.

"It's just that I never used it until I met you. I have to be very careful." She looked at him and saw that he didn't care for her reasoning. She sighed. "The Watergate is one of many spells I know, but have only slight control of. I can get myself out, but to use it on someone else ... I...I don't trust my skill in it." She looked at him, ashamed. "I'm sorry."

He sighed after taking a sip. "Don't be." There was a long moment of silence. He avoided her eyes, making her feel as if she had been the one to take his arm. She swallowed nervously as she rose from the bed, flinching when she didn't get the look she usually got when she approached him bare. Her stomach shrank as he did what he could to avoid looking at her.

"Baelor, I'm sorry. I didn't want..."

"You didn't even try, Zola," he snapped. He pushed her away as she tried to approach him. "You didn't even offer."

"Baelor, please. Don't do this to me," she pleaded.

He glared at her. "I'm ready to turn in, do you mind?" he said hostilely. The look on her face made him regret his words, but his pride refused to let him admit that he didn't mean it.

"Baelor. I...I would free you in a heartbeat if I trusted my skills, Baelor!" she cried. "Forgive me for being..." She tried to hug him only to have him suddenly shove her away. She hit the bed with a loud thud.

"I don't want to hear it, Zola!" He shook his head as she got up slowly. "I thought you loved me, I thought you wanted me..." His anger vanished as she faced him, revealing the gash she'd suffered from his childish reaction. "Oh, Zola."

She wiped the blood away nonchalantly, gathering her clothing as he just stood there in horror.

"Zola."

"Don't worry," she said glacially. "I'm fine. Nothing a little time can't heal." She started putting on her clothes. It was now his turn to suffer the cold shoulder.

He tried to tend to her wound, only to have her threaten him with a show of the power she knew she could control. As she finished, he called her to stay, watching helplessly as she left.

Months passed, then a year, then a year and two months. The next time he saw her she was dying in his arms, holding a small struggling bundle in her own.

Antoinette J. Houston

CHAPTER FIVE

The water

Tyrus watched as the High Lord and Sire Baelor left the Comne. He found himself a little worried by the look Baelor gave but let it go; he had his own mission to accomplish.

Tirin watched as Tyrus approached her. She found her heart beating like it was going to jump from her chest and land at his feet as he drew closer. So handsome he was, no longer ashamed of how he looked. His soft curled hair was pulled partially up into a topknot and the rest flowing freely down his back. Those around her began to back away at his approach and she grew ashamed that he was coming for her. She pinched herself. How could she feel that way? These people were just now accepting her and already she was threatening to turn her back on the one who was most loyal.

"What does he want?" Kalin asked, annoyed. He started to smile until he saw the look on Tirin's face.

"I can't believe you just said that with his hearing as it is," she said warningly.

Tyrus smiled, showing off his fangs as he reached them. "Luckily for him it is not his company I want."

"I...I apologize for..." Kalin started as Tyrus towered over him.

Tyrus ignored him as he took Tirin's hand. "I must speak with you, Tirin."

Tirin excused herself and followed him away. She turned to watch the reaction as she left and felt embarrassed once again for being associated with him. She couldn't understand where it was coming from.

"Tirin, I must apologize for getting you into this," he started as they continued to walk.

"Into what?" she asked, confused. "You and Darec convinced me..."

Tyrus bowed his head shamefully. "I know what I did and it was for selfish reasons that I did it."

Tirin looked at him. "I don't understand."

He stopped walking. "I wanted you to prove your worth, for these pompous, spoiled, hypocrites to see how special you are. To receive...to be able to receive a gift that..." He took another breath and watched as she smiled coyly at him.

"I understand now." She scratched her head. "Apology accepted and understood."

Tyrus sighed, relieved. "Now we can do whatever you want. You are not obligated to stay. I will escort you to wherever you want to go. Even to Wonderlost."

"Why would I go to Wonderlost?"

"I can honestly say that I do not know. I lose your scent every time."

She grinned. "So it was you."

Tyrus gazed at her, his eyes not moving from hers.

"The shadow that followed me." She started swaying from side to side with the music. "But I'm fine."

"But..." he started.

Tirin silenced him with a finger to his lips. "I know what can happen and strangely I want to see it through. I think." She took a deep breath. "Even if I was to leave now, or when I had planned, I would still have to deal with it when I returned. So I may as well take it like an adult here and now."

"I was really looking forward to visiting your hiding place in Wonderlost."

She grinned sweetly and laughed. "There you go being selfish again." She watched as he smiled widely. "What a gorgeous smile," she whispered unconsciously, to her own surprise. He started to say something in response when she cut him off.

"Dance with me."

"Not a chance," he said simply.

She pouted and grabbed his hand. "You can smile for me but you can't dance with me?"

Tyrus' face reverted to its original state. "The smiles are nothing but slips." He pulled away gently. "Accidents of nature. You will probably never see another."

"Not if I have anything to do with it."

He looked at her as if daring her to try. "Your new friends are waiting for you and I am quite sure more than willing to dance with you."

"But I want to dance with you," she said, pouting again. "I'm sick of you alienating yourself."

"Did you see anyone interested in me?" He looked around. "I surely do not. In fact, there is not a soul interested…"

"There is one. Me," she said sternly grabbing his hand. "And you're refusing me."

Tyrus sighed, despite the wonderful warm feeling filling him from her answer. "Tirin…"

"I'll tell my father that you were trying to use me for personal gain."

Tyrus regarded her sternly. "Brat. All right, let us get…"

"Yet again, should I be jealous?" Darec asked as he appeared behind Tyrus. Both become quiet.

"Neither of you heard my approach so it must've been an involved conversation," he said calmly. "May I join in?"

"No," Tirin answered, tugging on Tyrus' hand. "We were about to dance."

Darec's eyes widened in amusement. "Really? Tyrus hasn't danced in over eight years! He's bound to trample your feet more than anything else."

She glared, willing him to shut up. "That is of no concern to me. I want to dance with him and he wants to dance with me."

Darec grinned. "Doesn't look that way." He shook his head as Tyrus gently pulled his hand free.

"Tyrus...I..." she started only to be silenced as he cupped her face with his hand.

"Perhaps another time," he said quietly. She shook her head and started to grab for his hand again when he bent over and kissed her cheek.

Darec's eyes narrowed as Tyrus lingered a little too long with his too-familiar gesture.

"Enjoy your Comne, Cattea," Tyrus whispered before pulling away.

Tirin watched in disappointment as he disappeared into the crowd. Her hand caressed the spot where he'd kissed her. She wasn't sure of his intentions, nor was she sure of what she was feeling for him now. Maybe she was reading too much into it, but then Tyrus didn't express himself as others did and it was hard to understand him. He may have even thought of her as a sister he had to protect at all times.

Darec watched as she hugged herself. What was wrong with Tyrus? What was with this show? Never had he made a move as involved as this. Nonetheless, some emotionally retarded moron wouldn't outdo him. Tirin was going to be impressed with him enough to forget all about Tyrus' feeble attempt ... Darec paused. What was he concerned about anyway? Tyrus wasn't going to give a show of his true feelings anytime soon; it meant too much to him to keep them bottled up.

"Tirin…" He observed Tirin's glare.

"That was beyond rude, Darec," she snapped. "If I had been Tyrus I would have punched you in your mouth!"

Darec grinned slyly. "No, you wouldn't, and for that matter, neither would he."

She crossed her arms as she faced him. "I don't want to dance with you, that's for sure!"

"Tirin, c'mon! I didn't mean it to be mean, just a little friendly bantering. I didn't know it would be taken so literally." He took her arm gingerly. "If it will make you feel better I'll tell him I'm sorry next time I see him."

She refused to return his smile. "What do you want, my Lord?" She glared at him.

He sighed. "Well, to tell the truth, it was to ask you to dance, but I can see that you are no longer in the mood for that."

She smirked and agreed.

Darec shrugged. "Well since that's out of the question I can move onto the really important news."

"What important news?" she asked suspiciously.

The swell of horns and stringed instruments drowned out his answer as the time of the Barryn was upon them. Darec bowed deeply.

"Afterwards, we'll talk." He turned and headed toward his father, leaving her alone and confused.

Daynel Amforle watched Darec walk away from Tirin. She couldn't stand the little human whelp and found it more than irritating that she was getting so much attention. What was wrong with her people? Did they no longer see that the little human was conning them all? She flipped her crimson curls back, enjoying the feel of her pride and joy. It was the most luxurious red but it was also proof of her heritage. Her family was of a strong magykal background. Most were guardians for the Grand Ao'lean while others were high-level pyromages. She took another sip of her drink and watched Tirin become nervous. Daynel could admit that the girl had a good heart, but she was still human and this farce was more than insulting to her. To have a human contaminate the sacred ground of the Barryn just because she was raised here, as if she belonged, was ridiculous. True, the little human had inborn talents because of her mother, but she could be nothing more than a low-level charmer as her biological father probably had no ability at all. Daynel took another sip. Besides the only way the Grand Ao'lean would give her any type of gift was if Baelor happened to be her father. She frowned. She wouldn't put it past the old man to fall for a barbarian. Being held captive by them seemed to have made him less of an elf, or so her father said. She smiled slightly; her father said a lot of things about Sire Baelor in private but knew if the old Imperial found out, he would most likely be called out on it. Even with one arm, Baelor was still dangerous.

"Daynel?"

"Yes, Iilian," she answered vacuously. She turned to face the one girl who preferred to be a flunky rather than a friend. Although Daynel didn't mind, it was almost as if the girl was meant to be a servant rather than anything else.

Iilian fingered her ringlets as Daynel faced her. "You need anything? Daynel?"

The redhead shook her head then paused. "I wish for stronger drink, but that won't happen regardless of what you do."

Iilian nodded, eying the table where the grownups were. They were at a function that was to welcome them into adulthood, but were refused the drinks enjoyed by adults.

The music swelled and filled the city, inviting even those not attending the Comne to come and look on as two dozen of Ao'lean's youths were about to be deemed adults, and a few of them were about to be given more. Everyone seemed ready for the next step.

All except one.

As all eyes turned to her, Tirin felt like her body was slowly freezing over. Her eyes searched the crowd for her father. With every second that passed, more of her body seemed to ice over. Her panic-filled eyes met Darec's attempt at a consoling gaze. He mouthed that he was here for her, that everything was going to be okay. Not even the reassuring smile on his face was enough to make her feel better.

Tirin observed the Young Lord's smile shrink when footsteps approached her from behind. She knew immediately that they were not her father's.

She shook her head, the cold that crept over her limbs penetrating her body, making it even harder for her to swallow. "I–I can't do it, Tyrus." Her voice cracked. "I lied to myself...I...I should have left when you asked..."

"You can," Tyrus whispered soothingly, leaning in close. His hair brushed her cheek and immediately she knew that she wanted Tyrus. "I will be right here waiting for you."

He placed his hand on the small of her back and gently pushed her forward. The warmth of his hand spread through her, giving her the ability to move again.

Darec watched with a sour look as Tirin found her strength from Tyrus. The low buzzing he had experienced several times was now at its most annoying. It filled his head to the point where he couldn't think properly, and it was accompanied by an annoying metallic flavor that filled his mouth. He'd experienced it first when he'd had his way with Tirin.

Darec watched as Tyrus made his way back into the crowd. He never had understood how Tyrus had gotten Tirin to keep quiet about what had happened, or why he'd kept silent. Regardless of the past, neither had said a word to anyone and Darec was grateful. Yet now, he wondered, was Tyrus planning something?

Daynel watched, a little pleased when the smile on Darec's face faded as the dog came to the human's rescue. She'd never understood why Darec's distaste for the whelp changed so dramatically. How did his hate for her turn into adoration? Why her? Daynel glared at Tirin as she finally reached the rest of them to stand in front of the gates to the inner garden. Daynel's family was highly respected. Her blood housed a never-ending promise of magyk. If anyone were a perfect match for Darec, status wise, it would be her. And yet the Young Lord mooned after a crippled elf's adopted human whelp.

Tirin tried hard not to look up. She didn't want to meet any of the eyes she knew were on her. How embarrassing! Freezing like that and holding everyone up. Someone brushed up next to her, forcing her to look up. Kalin smiled at her and she couldn't help but smile back. She was pleased that he was determined to be there for her, that he wanted her attention. Tirin looked away from him and immediately her eyes locked with Darec's. The look on Darec's face was hard to discern. His smile seemed genuine, yet his eyes seemed to be unable to remove themselves from Tirin's. She almost felt as if he thought she was betraying him. The expression disappeared quickly as he realized she was looking at him and he moved forward from his post as practiced. The bowl in his hands gave a small whine when his grip tightened around its edges.

"Beyond these gates is the history of Ao'lean," he began stiffly. "Not all of you will be able to pass beyond the gate itself and those who do may not receive a gift, or a vision. But know that your being summoned here is more than most can say." Darec stood silent for a moment then closed his eyes and cocked his head sharply to the side like he was in pain.

Deimiyon started to ask if he was all right but stopped as Darec took a deep breath, shrugging away whatever was bothering him.

"In this bowl," Darec continued, "I have water from a spring that wells up from the center of the Grand Ao'lean. This is Water of Unlocking. Whatever is hidden away will be found and brought to light within you." He paused and stared at Kalin. "Be prepared as not all things brought out will be what you want."

Darec stood at the center of the chosen few. "My father holds twenty-four divining stones. If you are to proceed the stone will turn black; if not, the stone will remain white."

Without prompting, Deimiyon made his way to stand near his son and both of them waited for the first of the twenty-four to start the parade. For a moment, no one moved, and then with a disgusted sigh Daynel quickly made her way toward the High Lord. She grabbed a small satchel from the bowl he held then sauntered over to where Darec stood. He handed her a small cup and she delicately dipped from his bowl. She flashed him a dazzling smile, one that lasted all of two seconds, as his eyes didn't even see her. Daynel quickly drank the water, tossed the cup, and dumped the stone out of its pouch into her hand. The redhead looked up to see if Darec was even watching her progress and frowned because the Young Lord had turned away. She would be happy when Tirin showed how useless she was and how ridiculous it was for her to even be here.

Daynel turned to face the crowd when the water finally began to do as it was meant to do. The effects of the water varied from person to person, but it gave her a feeling of euphoria. Daynel's eyes held a glazed look as she gave a rather drunken smile before her stone flared and turned black. Immediately the redhead's eyes cleared and the silly smile vanished. The strange detached feeling she had earlier was gone without a trace.

Iilian went next and experienced the same euphoria, but her encounter seemed to last a little longer, meaning only that whatever ability she may or may not have was harder to locate. Kalin went next, his bravado bolstered by Iilian's success. He accepted his portion of water and received a glare from Darec that confused him.

"Young Lord, I--"

"You're holding up progress," Darec snapped.

Kalin quickly moved off to the side. All eyes were on him and he shrugged and downed his water quickly. After a few moments, a goofy smile made its way across his face and he dumped his stone out into his hand. The stone flashed immediately, but remained white.

The confident whispers disappeared quickly as Kalin looked at his stone. He gave a slight apathetic shrug, then bowed deeply before all of them. He made his way toward Tirin on his way back to the party.

"It doesn't matter that I don't have any magyk, it's not a real surprise." He smiled at her as she gave him a regretful look. "But if you dance with me afterward I'll feel better."

The buzzing in Darec's head hit a new tone as he watched Kalin whisper to Tirin.

The night wore on. Twenty-four potentials become sixteen assured. The last to make her way forward was Tirin.

All noise seemed to stop at once. Those who had failed stopped their displeased complaints and those who had succeeded curbed their excitement as Tirin slowly made her way to retrieve the last available stone.

Deimiyon gave her a reassuring smile as she reached in and took the last pouch. She held it to her chest tightly as she headed over to Darec. Before she could motion him to pass her the last cup, he took it upon himself to fill it for her.

"You have nothing to worry about," he whispered when she took the cup. She smiled weakly.

Tentatively she stood there, those who failed behind her and those who succeeded in front. With a nervous exhale, she moved the cup to her mouth.

Deimiyon watched warily as she drank the water, a sudden concern for her health flaring in his mind. Could she stand drinking the water? Even though she was half elf, what effects would it have on her?

The cup hit the ground with a sharp crack.

The High Lord moved forward as Tirin stiffened. The small satchel containing her stone dropped to the ground next as her hands went to her head.

"Tirin?" Darec asked, concerned. He watched her eyes roll to the back of her head. "Father...?"

Deimiyon dropped his bowl and rushed to Tirin's side.

Tirin couldn't understand what was happening. At first it was as if every pore of her being was opening up. For long agonizing moments, she could see everything around and beyond her, could smell every available scent, and could hear every sound being made. She inhaled and breathed with her whole body. In seconds, it all ceased and suddenly she found herself flying down a long, dark tunnel, with moving pictures surrounding her. Without a doubt, she knew these were her memories. Sound blared, almost deafening. But it was the memory ahead of her that intrigued her. No matter what she did, it raced further ahead. Something about it was forbidding yet her interest in it only increased. Unlike the others, it was blurred and elusive to the point of annoyance, but something pushed her to catch up with it. The fleeing memory was finally caught and without hesitation, she dove into it. Everything whirled about then suddenly stopped. Something running at her forced her to turn and face a younger Darec before he pressed something across her face. Everything went dark.

Deimiyon snapped his fingers loudly by Tirin's ear and smiled, relieved, as her eyes quickly refocused.

"You had us worried--" Darec started but cut himself off as she glared at him.

"Get away from me," she growled.

Deimiyon looked from his son to Tirin, a little confused by the sudden change of attitude. "Tirin? What is it?"

Her look of intense anger faded to be replaced with confusion. "I don't know…what am I doing?"

The High Lord bent down to retrieve the small satchel and placed it in her hand. Her shoulders dropped. "Oh."

The three of them stood together for a long moment. Tirin found that she didn't want to be here anymore. She definitely should have taken Tyrus up on his offer earlier. She wasn't sure if she wanted anything to happen, remembering the pros and cons of either possibility.

"Oh, reveal the stone already. We want to move on here," Daynel griped. "Show us what we already know so the rest of us…."

The High Lord cleared his throat sharply and narrowed his eyes at the redhead. The color drained from Daynel's face quickly.

Tirin turned the satchel over in her hand, keeping the material about the stone. As soon as the stone touched her skin there was a blinding flash.

The stone was black.

Daynel's mouth dropped open then shut quickly as Darec moved passed them to open the gate, ignoring the sudden swell of chatter of those gathered. Neither Lords gave them time to ask anything as they ushered the chosen through the entranceway.

The darkness within was profound at first then gradually their eyes adjusted. Millions of flash beetles blinked drowsily from the broad canopy of the Grand Ao'lean. The sound of water was finally heard in the tranquility of the Ao'lean's presence and one by one they all moved toward the center of the garden.

Tirin stood in awe for a moment before someone grabbed her.

"You're not special…you're just a plain human whelp that's…."

"Are you so insecure that you are willing to sacrifice your time with the Ao'lean?" one of the others interrupted.

"Leave her alone," someone else chimed in.

Daynel glared evilly into the darkness before releasing Tirin's arm and making her way over to the tree.

Tirin started to say thank you when something about the air changed. She turned and watched as one by one, the others fell under a spell. Each of them looked to be asleep where they stood. For long, drawn-out minutes she wandered around the Grand Ao'lean, feeling like she was being left out, that whatever was happening to the rest of them wasn't going to happen to her. She waited a little longer and then moved closer to the grand tree itself. Standing at its base, she felt compelled to touch it. She knew it couldn't awaken what was already awakened; she had magyk, magyk passed to her from her mother. But a vision, she could possibly receive that.

Her fingers brushed the body of the tree carefully, suddenly wondering if anyone had ever touched the tree itself. She looked around, seeing the others, even Daynel, as they remained more than a few meters away from the tree before becoming entranced. Tirin turned back around to the tree and place her hands flat against the body of it. The trunk was warm. She pulled away for a moment, realizing immediately that this tree was nothing like the ones beyond the gates. Tirin reached out again and replaced her hands upon the trunk. Beneath the normal-looking bark she could feel the swirling energy. Tirin was unable to remove her hands from the Ao'lean's body as she sank to the ground, the warmth she felt suddenly surrounding her, then everything seemed to fade.

When Tirin opened her eyes again she knew at once that she was in Wonderlost. She knew because of the tree that stood before her. The tree had been transformed into a house, originally belonging to the wizard that had enchanted Wonderlost. But now the tree house was different. It seemed new occupants had come to Wonderlost. She felt a twinge of irritation, but didn't entertain it.

The tree house had a new face, a garden blooming with flowers of all sorts, and new windows carved into it at higher levels, suggesting more rooms. That earlier twinge of irritation became slight jealousy. Someone was living happily here.

Then she noticed the bright red door opening. Two toddlers waddled out, both elven in appearance, twins, a boy and a girl. Their features were similar and yet drastically different. They noticed her and seem happier at her appearance. As the two children made their way toward her, they grew older. The girl had snow-white hair and brown eyes that reflected the light like an animal's. Her cheerful grin showed canines that were abnormal for her elfin heritage. She had a wild air to her. The boy had chocolate hair, violet eyes, and a shy way about him. As they drew closer they became teenagers, and the girl's countenance only grew wilder but her stature was cat-like, while her brother was more dignified, like he knew more than he was supposed to. Their teenage years quickly turned into young adults as they finally reached her. The boy bowed deeply, his features strong and regal. His sister followed his lead and now sported feline eyes, claws, and a tail. Upon rising, the girl called her Mother.

Tirin sat up abruptly, the vision fading fast, but the girl's voice seeming to echo through the darkness.

"Mother?" Tirin scratched her head, unintentionally causing her braided bun to fall. "Me?" The faces of the twins remained clear in her head. "Twins…elven twins…and mine?" Her heart raced as she tried to figure it out. Twins were definitely not common amongst elves, even fraternal twins, and the girl had white hair, not a color common in any race.

But.

The boy had violet eyes. Only one name came to her for that trait.

"Tirin?"

Trini suddenly realized that she had made her way out of the gardens and was back at the outside celebration. Kalin stood before her, smiling.

"Tirin, are you okay?"

"Yes…I'm fine…" She noticed the amused look on his face. "Why?"

He shrugged. "Who are Tylin and Theus?"

She froze. Were those their names? She felt as if her skin was on fire and knew she was blushing. Kalin snickered.

"My goodness, what was that for?"

"In my vision, there were--" she started, stopping when Kalin looked like he was choking.

"You had a vision?" He coughed. "The Grand Ao'lean gave you a vision?"

It was like he had slapped her in the face. Part of her was angry at herself for being surprised at his reaction. How could he go from hating her to truly believing in her in one night?

"You can't blame me for being surprised, Tirin," he said, grinning. "You're human; it's not something that's…"

"Yes, I had a vision, something that you will never experience, Kalin. Something more than a mere summoning to the garden." She watched, pleased, as his face flushed. "What did you think? That the Grand Ao'lean would actually summon me, a human, for no reason? That the Grand Ao'lean was showing me pity because of my blood?"

Kalin cleared his throat, trying to get her to lower her voice. "I'm sorry." He put his hands on her shoulders. "I wasn't trying to insult you—"

She slapped his hands away from her. "But you did," she snapped, then shook her head. "Never mind. Enjoy the rest of the celebration, Kalin." She started away when he took her hand.

"Good night, Kalin." She pulled away from him, even more irritated. He moved to stand in front of her.

"Tirin, c'mon. You have to see how…"

Darec approached from behind Kalin. "From the look on her face, I think that you have done something to upset her."

"Young Lord," Kalin said, without turning to face him. "I have done nothing to perturb her, right, Tirin?"

Before she could answer, Darec forced Kalin around. "You face me when you are speaking to me!"

Kalin glared at him then lowered his eyes. "I apologize for that, Young Lord," he said stiffly.

"I don't appreciate the tone of your apology, Kalin."

"Well, you would be just as resentful if I had barged my way into a conversation that did not concern me."

The surrounding conversations seemed to die away.

"Are you saying that I had no right to insert myself into your conversation with Tirin?" Darec narrowed his eyes at Kalin daringly. "You've insulted someone I care about and expect me to just stand idle?"

The whispers became shocked silence as everyone heard what Tirin heard. Tirin slowly pushed her way backwards through the increasing crowd of youths. Darec's words filled her with an anger that was cutting through her like a hot knife. The Water of Unlocking had opened her eyes to a memory that had been hidden away. Something that had lain within her all this time, explaining the irritation she had always had for the Young Lord but never understood why, until now. And with his telling everyone that he 'cared' for her not only embarrassed her, but also brought up hatred she had never entertained for anyone in her life before.

"I expected you to stay out of a situation that could have straightened--" Kalin snapped, stopped only when Darec punched Kalin square in the face.

Tirin didn't wait around for the full result of Darec's impulsive action. She immediately headed toward the outer garden and made her way deep into it, moving far enough away so the sounds of the celebration became muted to near silence. She wanted to scream, but she didn't think she was far enough away that she wouldn't alarm the guards. She never thought that tonight could turn out this way. This night had been seen two different ways in her head, but never like this.

Tirin slowly walked toward one of many ornate benches that were randomly placed throughout the garden. She stopped before it and stared off into the darkness. Where was her father? Why wasn't he here to comfort her?

"Tirin?"

She flinched at his voice and started to walk away when Darec grabbed her arm. "I'm sor--"

"Get your hands off of me!" she snapped. She watched as he dropped his head.

"I know my actions were childish…what I did was uncalled for, but--"

The glare alone was enough to tell him that something else was causing this reaction.

"I don't care." She turned her back to him. "I don't care what you do."

It was as if the world had paused, waiting for her next motion or words. Even the faint clamor of the Comne had vanished totally.

"What's with this attitude?" The confusion he felt was justified, but something told him that her anger with him was as well. The response she had given him at the Barryn ritual reminded him of that. An alarm went off in his head.

"The Water."

It was as if he could feel her hatred all of a sudden. The way she looked at him, her once neat appearance now a threatening one.

"I remember," she growled. "I remember what you did."

"I don't truly understand…wait." Was this why neither of them had said anything to his father? Because somehow after that hellish spell she started to cast went amok, she had somehow forgotten? Now he understood why she hadn't said anything, and why Tyrus couldn't either. Tyrus couldn't mention it to anyone if the victim didn't recall the incident. But the water, the water had unlocked it. Darec felt a bolt of ice run through him. Had Tyrus known this was going to happen? Was this why he no longer acted like an emotionless statue? He had to redirect the conversation, do something to keep her mind occupied till he could come up with a way to solve this new problem.

"Why are you still here? Why are you fawning all over me thinking that I'm going to be---?"

"Sire Baelor is your true father."

The aspens tried hard to get their attention, rustling their leaves in the night breeze. They went ignored.

Her eyes showed something clicking in her mind. This was a possibility she had considered once before but always brushed off.

"What?" she asked breathlessly, sitting hard upon the bench now behind her.

"I overheard my father telling your father that you had been summoned. You know only Ao'lean elves can be summoned, that the Ao'lean will only speak to those of Elvin blood…" He paused as she suddenly looked as if she was having difficulty breathing.

"I don't believe you."

"Sire Baelor didn't believe it either. He's probably still wrestling with it now." Darec shook his head. "The thought that he had adopted his own blood-related daughter sent him reeling."

"Shut up." She wilted against the bench, her eyes filling with tears.

"I figured you would want to know as soon as possible…so, well, that's what I was going to tell you earlier."

"You ass!" she shrieked, flying from the bench and raising her fists against him. *"You stupid, stupid ass!"*

"Whoa!" He caught her by her wrists, struggling a little to keep her strikes from landing.

"How could you think that I would want to know *from you?*" She struggled with him for a minute more before giving up. She fell against him and buried her face in his chest. "I hate you, I hate you so much."

"Really?" he asked, bemused, releasing her wrists to cup her face. "Something tells me otherwise."

She rolled her eyes and pulled away. "Well, you're wrong."

Darec grabbed her by her shoulders and pulled her back.

Tyrus watched from the path before finally reaching them just as Darec pulled Tirin close and kissed her. Without a word, he backed out quickly. The feelings he had held for so long were now boiling uncontrollably within him. He had to get out, to leave this place, before he did something he knew he would regret.

In his rush to leave he didn't notice Sire Baelor heading his way.

"Tyrus, have you seen Tirin?" The older elf was alarmed as the younger one brushed past him, growling. "Tyrus?" He watched as Tyrus quickly disappeared into the darkness beyond the plaza. Apparently the boy had seen something he hadn't wanted to. Baelor looked to the garden then headed toward it.

Darec released Tirin and smiled as she stood there quietly, the look on her face telling him nothing, but she wasn't angry anymo--.

Her hand snaked out and hit the left side of his face. He gawked and watched, too startled to move, as her other hand struck the other side of his face.

"Tirin!"

"You arrogant---!"

"Tirin?" It was her father's voice.

Tirin stood stiffly as her father walked up from behind Darec.

"I heard a slap…is everything okay?" he asked. Tirin stood there in an angry silence. "Cattea, is something wrong?" He touched her, surprised when she moved out of reach.

"Yes," she growled. "Get lost, Darec."

Baelor felt his throat tighten as he had a sinking feeling that he knew what was bothering her. He was definitely sure she was figuring out what he had come to tell her. She knew that no other being was able to receive a gift from the Grand Ao'lean. For a moment Darec didn't move, and then with an evil glare from Tirin, he bowed out and disappeared down the path into the darkness.

"All this time I thought that I was privileged…or special." She continued to avert her eyes. "Of course, I always knew what I was in the eyes of the people here…and dealt with how they treated me in stride."

Baelor swallowed; he knew where she was going. "Tirin, I…"

She looked up at him sharply. "All this time, Father…my life could have been more tolerable! Being seen as a half-breed would have been better than being seen as a pure-blood barbarian!"

"Stop that, right now!" Baelor snapped. "You are far from being a barbarian of any sort. Your being human does not mean that you are any less of a being than any other."

"But that's just it, isn't it?" She glared at him. "I'm not human! I'm not an elf either!" she shouted.

Baelor looked away from her. "Tirin, I'm sorry you had to find out this way…"

"Through Darec I found out!" She laughed. "Is that how you planned it?"

Baelor covered his face. That was what the little brat was doing. "He must've overheard…I can't believe…"

"If you didn't want him to tell me why didn't you tell me yourself?" she snapped. "Why did I have to find out from him?"

"You were supposed to hear it from me, not him." Baelor looked back the way Darec had gone, annoyed. "This was none of his concern."

"Well, it seemed that you weren't all that concerned about it either."

"I didn't find out about it until tonight!" he barked at her, growing angry with her attitude. He watched as her face fell as his words sunk in.

"You didn't know? How could you not?" Her voice wavered as she looked down at her hands. "I...Mother... she wouldn't have kept this from you...you should've known..." She moved further away from him.

Baelor scratched his head. "Cattea ..."

"Stop calling me that."

He sighed. "Tirin, when your mother placed you in my hands, you were mine. This changes nothing. Despite what you feel now, you know I love you, that no matter what, you *are* my daughter."

She looked at him. "By blood, Father. Not just because I was handed over to you by some random woman."

"Tirin, I'm growing tired of your attitude. I have apologized and will continue to until I feel you have forgiven me for my oversight, but don't forget that I am your..."

"What did you do to her?"

Baelor gawked at her.

"What did you do to my mother? Why would you not know about your own daughter?"

"That is way out of line, young lady!" Baelor bellowed, moving toward her. "Your accusations will stop now!"

"Not until I know the truth!" she yelled back even as she retreated. "I want to know what you did to her to make you feel so guilty that you felt you could redeem yourself by raising me." Her eyes locked with his as tears flowed. "Such guilt makes me wonder if you wouldn't have just left me the…"

Baelor slapped her.

"What you're saying to me is beyond disrespectful, Tirin. I will not have it!" He felt a twinge of guilt as she cupped her cheek. "I loved your mother, but things didn't work out as I wanted them to."

"How could you not see something like this? How could you not know?" Tirin looked at her father pitifully. "How could you keep this a secret not only from me but from yourself as well?"

Baelor blinked. "Secrets? You want to talk about keeping secrets?" He moved toward her. "How about your being pregnant?"

Tirin almost fell. He knew?

CHAPTER SIX

Time to leave

Darec practically shoved his fist into his mouth to keep himself from yelling out. She had been pregnant? He quickly stood up, feeling sick. He had to get out of there.

"How long are you going to hold that one, Tirin?" Baelor continued. "Yes!" he shouted. "I knew about that, too, and still you refuse to say anything about it!"

He looked at her. "When you came to me complaining of stomach pains, remember that?" He grabbed her by her arm and shook her a little. "The physician told me what was wrong. I didn't want to believe it, but he pointed everything out to me. I told him to keep quiet as I wanted to hear it from you." He released her. "That was seven years ago, Tirin! Seven!"

Tirin couldn't believe that all this time he'd known and said nothing. She didn't know what to do, what to say.

"You weren't ever going to tell me, were you?" He watched as his daughter slowly shook her head. They were silent for only a few seconds before hearing a long eerie howl far off in the distance.

"You should've come to me, you should've let me help."

Tirin stood there in silence, wringing her hands as he calmed.

"You should've given me the chance to help. What happened, happened, and there's nothing we can do about that, but for you to keep...my...grandchild away from me..."

"I had no choice..." she whispered, trying to think up a way to explain to him what she could remember.

His eyes widened quickly, almost threatening to pop from his head. "No choice? Y-you were raped?" He grabbed her again, forcing her to face him. "Why would you keep something like that a secret, Tirin? Why would you keep it from me?" He allowed her to pull away from him.

"Father..." The word rape echoed through her like a giant bell. A couple reasons popped into her mind why she couldn't tell him what had truly happened then. He wouldn't believe her for one. Yes, he knew she had abilities, but as far as he was concerned it wasn't anything substantial. Then there was the fact that he was best friends with the High Lord. Being told that she had been taken advantage of by his best friend's only son meant that he would have to confront him on it, and that meant bloodshed as far as honor amongst those of the warrior class. She hated that she was actually protecting Darec.

"Did he threaten you? To keep you from saying anything?"

"Father..."

"Does he live here?" Baelor's mind suddenly swam with faces of young elves that could be possible suspects. "Is he close by?"

"Father, I wasn't raped." She paused.

He stood there like a statue. "What?"

Tirin tugged at one of her braids. "I wasn't raped."

He was flustered; his face turned red as he paced in front of her. He stopped abruptly, startling her a little as he seemed to be fighting with his words.

"Are you..." He choked and closed his eyes as he tried again.

Tirin sighed. "You wouldn't understand or worse, wouldn't believe me if I told you."

"Were you just so in love that you had no choice or are you telling me that you just didn't…"

"Father."

"Don't 'Father' me!" he bellowed. "You were barely thirteen!" He paced in front of her. "I thought for sure that I raised you better than this!"

Tirin looked at him, not sure what to do next.

"What's his name?"

"Who's?" Tirin asked, genuinely confused.

Baelor rolled his eyes. "The father! What's his name?"

She backed off as he moved toward her. "There is no father."

"So he's dead?" he spat. "This was his last wish or something?" He looked at her incredulously. "To get a mere child pregnant?"

Tirin shook her head. "No, there is no father!"

"Don't protect him! It doesn't make your situation any better," he growled.

"My situation?"

Baelor continued to pace. "I thought I could trust you, Tirin. Trust you enough not to betray me…"

"I haven't betrayed you! You're making this worse than it is!" she yelled. Baelor glared at her and she fell silent.

"Why did you hide this? I could have helped; we would've gotten through this together!"

"You wouldn't believe me, Father," she pleaded.

He threw his hands up, exasperated. "Stop telling me what I would've done!" he seethed. "What do you think I am, an idiot? Whether I believed it or not, I would've done all that I could for you."

She stomped her foot. "Fine, I'll tell you! It was a spell! I tried a spell of revenge and forgot a major component, thinking that it didn't matter if I had it or not so it made up for it by changing…"

"Stop it!" Baelor snapped. "Are you trying to tell me a spell got you pregnant?"

Tirin kept her eyes locked with his. "Yes."

"Leave! Get out of my sight, girl!" he growled.

"But I was trying to tell you the truth! I told you, you wouldn't…I just…" she sobbed.

"Leave! I don't want to see you right now. I don't want to hear you!"

Tirin covered her mouth as he turned his back to her. Tirin turned and ran off.

Baelor covered his face as he listened to her footsteps fade.

Tirin felt unsteady as she rejoined the celebration. She was approached dozens of times to dance, but all she could think of was to get out of there. She didn't feel well and the closeness of the crowd was irritating her. Tyrus would help her. She looked around for him, her chest tightening as it began to appear that Tyrus had left. She cursed Darec for his interference and his selfishness.

"Tyrus!" she yelled. "Ty…" Someone grabbed her by her shoulder, turning her around.

Daynel stood there, a sour look on her face. "So you think you're special."

Tirin waved her away and started looking for Tyrus again only to have the redhead grab her again.

"Daynel, I don't …"

"I didn't ask for your attention, human, I'm demanding it. As someone who truly belongs here, I just wanted you to know that no matter what happened to you in there, you are still a barbaric human and nothing, not even the Grand Ao'lean, can change that," she snapped.

Tirin lost her patience and shoved her away. "Tyrus!" she screamed.

Illian stood beside the shocked Daynel, her hands placed defiantly upon her hips. "I saw your canine friend take off for the main gates. He was very upset about something when he came back from the Garden."

Tirin stared at her in disbelief. Tyrus was in the garden? She covered her face with her hands. He must have seen the kiss then.

Daynel watched as the human looked as if she was going to burst into tears, but Daynel did not care. She moved Illian out of the way.

"I didn't appreciate that, cur," she hissed. "Don't expect to get away with…"

Tirin screamed. "Get away from me!"

The ground began to tremble and everyone stopped their chattering as a deep rumbling soon followed the trembling. Tirin felt a sudden release of pressure through her chest and watched as the ground reacted like water when a pebble was dropped into it. The ground settled only after the last wave. The party was ruined and the people were more than frightened, as no one knew what had just happened or what had caused it. Daynel looked for Tirin, her anger with the girl silenced, but she was nowhere to be found.

Tirin ran as hard as she could, sure that they would all soon be after her. She had to leave before they got themselves together; she had to leave anyway with the way she'd spoken to her father. She pinched herself; she needed to get control of her emotions! What happened back there was an effect of her anxiety. That couldn't happen again, she couldn't let it.

In what seemed like seconds, she reached home, her heart in her throat as she looked behind her, expecting to see a throng of people following her.

"Tyrus!" Tirin screamed as she rushed into the house. "Tyrus, please!" Tirin stumbled as the heel of her boot finally gave out. She kicked them off as she ran up the stairs to his room, knowing he wasn't there before she opened the door. She fell to her knees, the urge to cry strong, but she refused.

She slowly stood up and headed to her room, closing the door quietly behind her. She had to get out of here, go somewhere else. She looked around her room. It was time for her to try and make a life for herself beyond Ao'lean.

CHAPTER SEVEN

humans

Darec dragged Kalin's body to the cellar of an abandoned house. He almost smiled at his cleverness and the superstitious nature of his people. This house used to be Tyrus' home, left alone since the night of his mother's death. No one wanted to awaken the spirit of his mother. They feared that she may be angry at not only what happened to her, but also what was done to her son. No one wanted to risk being haunted.

Darec watched the boy's body flop about as it tumbled down the stairs. It had been no different than killing a dog. He watched the body land in a broken heap at the bottom of the stairs, shielding from view the carcasses of the animals that had fallen victim to his sick hobby. He didn't know why he did it, he just knew it made him feel…wonderful. Darec closed the door and stood there for a moment. Why didn't it bother him that he had just taken the life of another elf? He rubbed the back of his neck. It had been so easy, barely a struggle. Kalin was more gullible than he had thought.

Kalin had actually thought that Darec was genuinely sorry for what he'd done. That he was going to take him to the castle to retrieve payment for his humiliation. Darec smiled. He had no regrets. With ease, he was able to get Kalin to trust him enough to follow him. For five minutes, they walked away from the celebration toward a dark alleyway. Darec moved in and out of the shadows until Kalin actually thought he had lost the Young Lord. Darec then appeared behind the clueless moron and shoved him, causing him to tumble forward. Kalin yelled out and started to curse him, but even he knew he was in trouble when Darec put his hands around his neck. In a well-practiced move, Darec broke the young elf's neck with no problem.

Darec headed back toward the front door, that annoying little voice at the back of his head whispering about something. He used to know what the voice was saying, but as time went by, it became more mysterious. It was drowned out by that incessant buzzing that only quieted when he killed something. He knew it told of something important, something he should be concerned with.

As he drew closer to the Comne he could hear the alarmed commotion. He slowed and watched from a position out of sight; the party was in havoc. The area was a mess. Whatever had happened was major and yet apparently unknown as the people wandered about confused. He looked up the hill toward his own home and just barely caught sight of someone entering the Desgjin estate. He watched as the lantern in Tirin's room was lit and she passed in front of her window. He was quite sure she was on the verge of hysterics and in need of a comforting shoulder. Tyrus was nowhere to be found apparently, as he could hear her scream for him.

Tirin finished dressing and at the same time she brought her packing to a close. Her heart was in her throat as her mind replayed the look on her father's face. He hated her! She had no idea where she was going to go or how she was going to survive…wait, she had Wonderlost. She felt only a tiny bit better. She would be out there all alone, but she would still be close to Ao'lean. No one would know where she was or how to get to her even if they wanted to find her. She sat down on the bed, feeling dizzy again. She'd caused an earthquake in the square; she was quite sure they all knew it was her. They would be coming for her, she knew it, along with her father. She covered her face as the tears finally started to fall. Why was this happening?

The front door creaked open slowly and she stood up quickly. Sure that it was her father, she tied her bag shut and headed to her window.

"Tirin!" Darec shouted.

Tirin froze, one leg out over the ledge. She gripped her bag tightly, then found it hard to leave. She had to make him understand how much she appreciated his interference.

Darec was relieved to see her come back in, sure that she was going to hurt herself. She walked over to him and he opened his mouth to say something when she slapped him and then started to hit him again, stopping when he caught her hand.

"Tirin, enough of this childish crap! Why are you attacking me?"

"Why?" She stared at him incredulously. "You interfere in affairs that don't concern you and you want to know what that was for? You deserve more for what you've done!"

Darec quickly backed off, not wanting her to hit him again. "I thought it would be happy news, something you would appreciate…"

"I would have appreciated it if it had come from my father's own lips!" she shrieked. "What were you think…no, you already said it." She paced in front of him.

Darec looked around the room for something clsc to talk about, then realized that she had a bag draped over her back and her clothing had changed.

"What are you doing?"

She paused for a second, not realizing what he was talking about, then remembered. She twirled, arms out.

"I'm leaving, what does it look like?"

He swallowed. "It looked like you've lost your mind," he said, moving to grab a hold of her. "Your father…"

She moved back toward the window. "My father told me to leave, that he didn't want to see me anymore," she lamented. "That was my fault, the way I treated him, spoke to him. I blame you for the reaction I gave him."

"He didn't really mean it and you know it!" he said, moving again. This time he froze as she glared at him, her hand out.

"Back off! This is your fault! Why don't you apologize?"

"I thought I was doing you a favor."

"Well, you weren't! All you were concerned with was helping yourself!"

Darec looked at her. "How?"

She shrugged. "How am I supposed to know your plan?"

They remained quiet for a few moments before she shook her head and started for the window again.

"There is no plan, Tirin. I wasn't trying to…"

She shook her head. "I don't care for any of your excuses, Darec."

He sighed. "But where are you going? Who's going to take care of you?"

She gawked at him, almost laughing at his attempt at concern.

"What does it matter?"

"Because I want to do it."

She appraised him suspiciously. "Do what?"

"Marry you."

She felt her stomach fall to the floor as her mouth dropped open. Had he just proposed to her?

"Tirin?"

She stared at him in utter disbelief. The audacity of his arrogance! How could he possibly make his mouth say this to her?

She was surprised at the feelings boiling up inside her and relieved by the reaction she was about to give him.

"Tirin?"

"I should've killed you when I had the chance."

Darec balked as she hissed at him, momentarily unable to move or think as her words sank in. Finally, he did move for her and watched, alarmed, as she ducked out the window.

"Tirin! No!" he yelled, thinking that she was trying to kill herself. He felt utterly stupid as she climbed down the tree outside the window. He watched as she disappeared beyond the property and slammed his fist against the ledge of the window, that strange buzzing filling his head again.

How dare she refuse him? And then threaten his life? Was she out of her mind? Did she not realize what he could do to her? He took a deep breath and headed out of her room quickly; he had to catch up with her.

Tirin didn't feel the tears until she was almost halfway to the main gates. She was livid with disgust. How in the world could he make himself think that she could actually consider him as a lifemate? Was he that conceited? Of all the nerve, to think that she could possibly forgive and forget…she growled as she rounded a corner, pausing momentarily as she wiped her face. She had never growled like that before. It had sounded a like a true animal. She sounded a lot like Tyrus. She shrugged it off as the gates loomed before her. She wished that Tyrus had been there so she could explain and smooth things over with him. Well, that and watch him beat Darec to a pulp for his impertinence.

The two guards at the gates walked toward her, large smiles on their faces as they stopped her.

"An' where d'you think yuir goin', lady?" the older one asked, grinning.

Tirin looked at him pleadingly. "Just this once, Zeph, let me through...I..."

"Tirin, darlin'," the younger one started. "All this time you've been sneakin' out and this time you actually ask us to leave? What's wrong?"

"I really don't have time to explain, Rane, please, just let me through!" She didn't understand why she'd come this way either. She could have been well on her way if she had just taken her usual route out.

"Now, you know we can't. It's not safe anyway. There's a band of hunters out there now...lost due to the Ao'leans, they could..."

The sound of hooves spun her about, as she knew who it was. Darec was racing his horse, Necrom, toward them like the devil was after him. Tirin grabbed their hands.

"Open please!"

Both of them looked at her warily. She seemed scared as their Young Lord approached.

"What's goin' on?" Zeph asked sternly.

"Tirin!" Darec called.

She became frantic as he drew closer and the guards continued to ignore her plea.

"Ohh! Fine!" she snapped. She clapped her hands together in front of her, then raised them over her head. As her hands moved upwards so did she, up and over the gates.

Darec reined his horse to a near crashing halt. Both he and the guards stood there and watched her fly away over the Gateway.

"Open the DAMN GATE!" Darec ordered. They moved quickly to start the mechanisms.

Tirin wished she could have time to enjoy this new use of her levitation spell but could feel it draining her quickly as she tried to prolong its effectiveness. She flew a foot or two above the ground, following the path to Ao'lean Forest. She pushed her spell and watched as inch by inch she got closer to the ground. The spell dispersed altogether when she reached the deepest part of the forest. The high rate of speed she had picked up sent her crashing into a tree as she fell from the air. She righted herself quickly as she heard the thundering of Darec's horse. Tirin steeled herself against the pain. The breathtaking agony in her side informed her that she may have broken something; hopefully, at worst she had only bruised a rib or two. She gritted her teeth and started running, trying to reach the edge of the forest before Necrom reached her.

"Okay! Okay! I won't take you back!" Darec yelled as he circled in front of her. He saw the cuts on her face and the way she was holding her ribs. "Tirin, c'mon, you're hurt, let's not..."

Necrom moved back as she raised her hand toward him. Tightly holding her side, she wished she knew more attack spells. As it was, the pain was too much of a distraction for her to control the potency. She wished she had practiced that levitation spell more. It took almost everything she had. She could throw sparks at him but a good lightning spell was what she wanted. She swallowed painfully. Her chest was on fire from the run. She hoped he believed her bluff.

"Tirin," he said warily. "Even I know that you're not that advanced. You used a lot of energy with that escape of yours." He swallowed. Despite his own magykal knowledge, she could still hurt him if she really wanted to. "If you cast another spell you'll more than likely pass out."

She kept her arm rigid as she backed away from him slowly. How she hated that he was so knowledgeable.

"Tirin. I'll...I'll take you to the edge of the forest."

Her hand lowered a bit.

"I...don't...believe you," she panted. "Why?"

He relaxed a little. "I know I've gone about this all wrong...and that there's more than likely nothing I can do to change your mind. You are stubborn." He cleared his throat as they locked eyes. "I want to do something right for once…for you. As long as you promise to be careful and at least come back one day…"

She lowered her hand abruptly to plant it on her hip.

"What a pile of lies!" she snapped. "You proposed to me, Darec! To me! What makes you think that I would say yes? Because you're a Lord?"

Darec shook his head. "No! I proposed because I love you…because I want you as mine!"

Necrom retreated a few steps more when she growled at him. "I know you, Darec! Underhanded motives are your specialty!"

They stood there in silence for a long time before he sighed and looked up at the sky. He put his hand out for her to take.

"I will take you to the edge of Ao'lean Forest. I promise not to do anything suspicious."

Tirin swallowed as she looked at his hand. She couldn't get anywhere in her condition. "Okay, but I'm warning you. If we end up back in Ao'lean…I'll…I'll tell."

Darec glared at her, knowing where she was going but not quite believing that she was trying to blackmail him.

"Tell what?"

"I'll tell your father what you did to me." She watched as he became impassive.

"Why would you do that?" he asked, trying to ignore the buzzing in his head.

"Because I hate you," she said simply, fighting the smile that threatened but enjoying the feeling of finally being free. The muddled emotions she had for him earlier were gone. It was Tyrus she wanted, not this spoiled brat. She looked back toward Ao'lean. Tyrus would know where to find her. "I've always hated you but I just couldn't remember why. If it weren't for Tyrus you would be dead. You should thank him when next you see him." She searched him carefully for a reaction and was surprised as he did nothing but chew his lip.

"Understood," he responded and they were quiet again. He stared at her with that same look he'd given Kalin before he hit him. She massaged her side.

"I have one question, then we can go," he said coldly.

"What?"

"Was the child mine?"

She laughed loudly then subdued it as her ribs pained her. "I knew it! I knew it! The true reason you had the audacity to ask that ridiculous question! Because you loved me, HA!" She glared at him and watched alarmed as his face contorted.

"Was the child mine?" he barked. She quieted.

"No."

He doesn't seem fazed by the answer at all as he sat upon Necrom a moment before gesturing for her hand.

She looked at him for a few seconds, unable to rid herself of the feeling that she was putting herself into danger. She took his hand, he helped her mount behind him, and they headed for the edge of the Forest.

Ten minutes passed and suddenly Necrom reared violently. Tirin screamed as she tried to hang on. She assumed that Darec was going to grab for her, but instead he allowed her to fall. Darec watched her land with a sickening thud and she laid still. He circled around her, Necrom's hooves coming close to stepping on her. The guards would be here sooner or later; their warning of the human hunter was enough to warrant quite a few of them as their Young Lord wandered the dark forest for Tirin. He smiled as the cause of her death came to him. The humans did it. They saw her as a traitor to their kind and killed her and he found her too late.

Darec reared Necrom up over her only to find himself propelled from his horse. He yelled out as he saw the arrow protruding from his upper arm. It had gone straight through! He looked around and saw the owner of the arrow lowering his bow. He was hoping not to run into them so soon! He reached for his weapon only to realize he was not armed. Comnes required there be no weapons, as the Grand Ao'lean despised them, and he hadn't thought to arm himself before he left. He watched as five humans surrounded him and the unconscious Tirin.

"Dou vere urd, Dale, jo de en human."

Darec looked at the speaker, his strawberry-blonde hair pulled back, revealing his scruffy face, marred and cut from their lengthened visit in Ao'lean Forest.

"Ja kin der bledere kure jout ler sis gourbuneer voods."

Darec watched as two men who looked to be siblings, with complexions like Tirin's, dismounted and started for him. He retreated, tripping over Tirin.

The young blond of the group glared at him. *"Kin joutan nix'jah predo jouta'er finis con'jah? Bor garlinin gar mero si'dok."*

The one called Dale looked at him with a strange grin on his face. *"Nader de dani ni urma o rouist? Ni, Malik, jouta'la saburk jaha atur, re'nir vunt e ando un gar bor nixin en elf eh mirs e ar un ernada sis erdi cam."*

Darec watched the two talk, saw the little one motion toward him. He knew they were threatening him but he couldn't understand a word they spoke, which only made his panic worse. He started screaming.

"Help! Help, we're here! We're...ughn!" One of the darker ones hit him in the stomach, then knocked him down.

"Dale, ret dou aver viruk o joutan kin ... "

It was the distant sound of more hooves heading their way that caused Malik to jump down and retrieve Tirin. Darec yelled for him to leave her, only to be hit across the face before the five hunters took off. Minutes later Zeph, Rane, and four others appeared, Zeph dismounting before his horse to a halt.

"Lord Darec!" Zeph motioned for the other four to go after the hunters as he and Rane helped the Young Lord. "What happened?"

Darec wiped his face and shook their hands away as they tried to steady him. He looked in the direction the hunters had gone.

"I finally caught up with Tirin when those hunters surrounded us…"

Zeph looked around as he caught his breath. "Lord Darec, where is Tirin? Did she get away?"

Darec looked at him, then shook his head. "They took her."

Antoinette J. Houston

CHAPTER EIGHT

Courage

Tyrus ran to the edge of Noir Swamps non-stop from the Comne.

The picture of Darec with his fingers entangled in her hair, with his lips pressed against hers, burned like acid in his mind. Tirin was not meant for Darec; he would only hurt her in the end. He looked up and howled at the pale moon, its glowing body encircled with a halo. It was a phenomenon said to mean a time of revelations and trials. Tyrus laid upon the ground, breathing deeply as his body screamed for rest, his lungs on fire from the long run. After a few moments, he stood and faced the swamps as he had so many times before.

"You have to get her to remove the curse!" he snapped at himself. "I have to face her."

Reluctantly his feet obeyed and slowly he entered.

The darkness was profound and at first, he found himself blinded by it. Gradually his eyes adapted, the moonlight reaching within the swamps when the sun could not. The sounds of the swamp were as eerie as he remembered. The trees themselves seemed to warn him of his choice, looking as if they had once been humanoid beings. The knolls on some resembled pain-stretched faces, their lower limbs outstretched arms wanting for help. Tyrus found that fear was a great cure for anger. The thought that touching one of these horrible trees would transform him into one of them chilled him. With some difficulty, he moved through the swamp. Firm ground gave way to quagmire and he soon began to regret his rashness in coming here. His feet moved clumsily forward yet they picked up their pace as the trees seemed to reach for him anyway, their branches catching and snagging his hair and clothes. The wail of whatever animals that dared to live here only made his pulse race faster. His mind began to create reasons for him to turn around. With each step threatening to pull his boots off, he realized that his idea to come here at this time might have been a rash decision. He was far from prepared and appearing so late on Bayne's doorstep resembling the usually mud covered and bedraggled, eyeless mirecats would not give a good impression. His cape caught on the limb of a struggling bush and with impatience he ripped it from around his neck. He stopped, realizing he was only complaining to convince himself to turn around.

"I am not turning around," he told himself. "I am going to go through with this." He peered behind him and saw that he had come too far to even consider turning back.

Bayne lived in the dead center of the swamp, the most dangerous part of this dreary place as the muck and sludge was deeper there. Time seemed to slow down as he made his way toward the witch's hovel.

The sound of something large moved behind him.

Tyrus looked around him, paying the swamp more attention, forgetting the cold and the frightfulness of his surroundings. Something was following him. His violet eyes scanned the area, finding nothing. He sniffed the air and caught the scent of something strange. He had never smelled this variety of being before. Whatever it was, it wasn't a common animal.

The sound of a sword leaving its sheath reassured him that it was a humanoid being of some sort. He strained his eyes, forcing himself to find his would-be attacker. Discomfort on the very edge of pain arose briefly in his chest, distracting him for a moment. Tyrus almost smiled. His attacker was going to get the shock of its life.

It moved as if it was nothing but a shadow. He observed it before having to flatten himself into the muck, dodging the blade of a monstrous sword. The tree behind him fell as it was cut in half. He turned quickly to face it and almost paused, a mistake that would have cost him his head. It turned out to be a she, a she that turned out to be a race of elf he had only heard of. She stood almost six feet in height, her svelte body almost hidden by her massive sword. Her white hair and pale, iridescent skin told of her Ferine heritage but her eyes said that she was mixed. They were a brilliant emerald green instead of the ginger-colored eyes he had read about. Ferine strength and agility was twice that of land elves but they were supposedly sensitive to sunlight and saltwater.

"Ferine," he said simply and watched, impressed at how easily she swung the blade upwards.

"No," she answered, her voice like thick syrup as she launched herself at him for another attack.

Her downward slash would have caught any other elf and he found himself somewhat relieved that he was in the process of changing. His increased agility allowed him to dodge her frighteningly quick attacks. He frowned as he realized that he was almost thankful for being cursed.

She growled with each swing. She had little trouble moving in this muck as she followed him, her blade not missing a chance to try and separate some part of his body from the rest of him. The tip of her blade nearly caught his shoulder when his legs buckled from their transformation. He side-stepped, letting her momentum carry her past where he had been to fall into what looked to be solid ground but was really a pool. He was slightly disappointed that she didn't seem surprised as his form changed, not even concerned when he undressed before her. Tyrus was unable to ponder why that was, knowing that her mud bath would be a short one. He loped off into the center of the swamps with her yelling after him.

She locked her glare onto him as she rose from the mud. Retrieving her sword, her eyes took on an eerie glow, and darkness seemed to coalesce around her until she vanished from sight.

Tyrus splashed through the mud, wondering if he would have come here had he known about the maniac Ferine. He knew the answer to that would have been no. There was no turning back now, though; she would skin him alive. Why was she here though? Was she Bayne's protection? Was she here on her own accord or was she in service to the witch?

A swift kick sent him flying into a deep pool and his enemy was there to meet him as he resurfaced. The pale elf appeared out of the darkness as if she owned it.

"Intrudah," she growled, jumping into the pool after him. "Ah will naht ahllow you to trespahss!" She cleared her blade from its sheath.

Tyrus growled fiercely, watching for a moment as she paused, then continued. He turned away only to have her grab his tail. He whirled about and snapped at her, and she released him quickly. With a loud bark, he threatened to latch onto her. She fell away from him, letting go as he came within centimeters of fusing his teeth with her flesh. Despite her tremendous skill, he could tell she had a fear of dogs. Tyrus faced her. She screamed in utter rage when he licked her and lost her footing, then her grip on her sword as he launched himself at her. He dashed out of the pool, leaving her behind again, and this time she screamed in utter hate. He looked behind him and watched her catch up with him. Holding her hands out, she was quickly surrounded by darkness. Like thick smoke it surrounded her, then it, and she, floated up like fog and flew at him at an alarming rate. He zigzagged through the brush; he had no time to waste.

The hovel loomed ahead; his goal was right in front of him. He barked loudly, knowing the old woman would come out to see what the commotion was about. This deep in the swamp, there weren't many things to make such a racket. He was surprised as he leapt upon the rotting porch to see that instead of the witch, a male elf came out to meet him.

The elf was tall and well built, with broad shoulders and a proud stature. Tyrus guessed that he had been living here for quite a while because his skin was a pale butter cream in color. Runic tattoos adorned his arms and shoulders, tapering off about his neck. His bright blond hair was stiffly braided into two braids down his back, showing off his pierced ears. The mystery elf's ice blue eyes stared at him and spoke of a character that had little patience with much as he stood straight after ducking through the doorway.

With a wave of a hand, Tyrus found himself suspended in the air. He was frozen in place as the new occupant of the house came out to investigate.

"Evergreen!" the elf shouted into the night. He jumped off the porch to meet the mud-covered and highly upset Ferine. The elf pointed toward the dog now floating over the porch. "A dog, Evergreen. A mongrel. Could you not keep it from disturbing me?'

Tyrus felt his tongue beginning to dry off as it hung out in the open air. He gagged as he made the attempt to speak.

The elf turned to face the dog, hearing the strangled sound. "That was not a sound a normal dog would make."

"Reelly," Evergreen grumped as she crossed her arms. "You ahctually think ah couldnae cahtch ah dog?"

The elf moved closer to Tyrus, giving him a closer look. There was something familiar about him.

"It used to be ahn elf, ahn Ao'lean elf from the clothing he 'ad been wearing," she explained as she began scraping some of the mud from her own clothing.

Tyrus fell to the porch with a surprised yelp and watched as the elf stood over him threateningly.

"Who are you and what do you want?" he demanded.

Tyrus was about to answer when he realized that he did recognize the elf's voice. The body had changed, drastically, but the voice had not.

"Alce?"

Alce stepped back, his eyes narrowed in high suspicion.

"Don't make your situation worse than it is. Tell me who…"

Tyrus sat back upon his haunches. "It is I, Tyrus Raylok."

Alce laughed, then became silent as he inspected the wolf closely. The only thing recognizable was the dog's voice and…his eyes. Alce remembered those eyes. Resentment raised its head as he remembered all the times that Darec and Tyrus abused him and he'd had to look into those eyes. They had been so cold then.

"Tyrus," Alce said, sure now. "Interesting. You're a dog."

"As observant as always." Tyrus frowned. "What are you doing here and where is Bayne?"

Alce leaned against the beam behind him, not sure if he should laugh or be wary. "Why should I tell you anything?" he asked arrogantly. "I owe you no favors."

Tyrus looked at him. "Alce, if it is the past you still live in, then you have the right to feel as you please, but I must see Bayne." Tyrus scratched his neck, knowing that he now had fleas. No matter the outcome of this day, Tirin was going to give him the 'bath of doom' if she caught him before he was able to coax his body to transform.

Alce smiled coldly. "How long have you been this way?"

Tyrus looked at him, annoyed. "I do not have time for this." Tyrus noticed Alce's eyes flash, changing from ice blue to amber. He paused.

"You will have all the time in the world if you expect any help here," Alce said haughtily as he fingered the end of one braid. "You do as I say, tell me whatever I want to know."

"Six years," Tyrus answered.

Alce beamed widely, ignoring the startled look at his sudden change in demeanor. He sat down on the porch.

"A year after I left, huh?" He sucked his teeth, shaking his head. "I missed all the excitement."

Evergreen watched as the dog's shoulders seemed to fall while Alce went on about how he deserved what he got, how it pleased him so much to see him begging him for help.

Tyrus' ears pricked up. "Beg you for help?"

The blonde considered him slyly and then nodded. He watched as Tyrus got to his feet.

"I do not want nor need your…"

Alce's amber eyes reverted to their ice blue color as he grinned. "Bayne's not here." He burst into laughter at Tyrus's reaction. Even though Tyrus' body was that of a wolf, he was very expressive. Alce delighted in how the animal's mouth hung open in disappointment, his tail drooped between his legs and his shoulders slumped. Alce paused. Tyrus was never this expressive when he was normal.

"What's wrong with you?"

"What is wrong with you?" Tyrus spat back.

Evergreen crossed her arms. "He's nahtheen like you described."

Tyrus looked at her then back at Alce as he shrugged. "I know, he's making it look as if I was lying." He looked at the wolf. "I don't appreciate that."

Tyrus felt as if he had swallowed a deadly rock toad, one where the poisons were so potent that it was turning his insides to slime. He shouldn't have waited so long to come see the witch. This was his punishment for being such a coward.

Alce watched Tyrus' turmoil with confusion. He found himself smiling slightly; he never thought he would feel sorry for one of the worst bullies he had ever had. He couldn't fathom what could humble one who at one time enjoyed tormenting others.

"He's in lahve."

Both Tyrus and Alce looked at Evergreen, who just shrugged.

"It's ahbvious. Ahll the horrific theengs this boy hahs done to you, Ahlce, how you described him. It's gaht to be lahve thaht's changed 'im."

Alce grinned, turning from his Ferine companion to Tyrus, who turned away from him almost bashfully.

"Is it true?" he asked.

Tyrus looked at him plainly then started to jump off the porch. Alce grabbed his tail and quickly let go when Tyrus whirled about and snapped at him.

"I apologize for my intrusion," he growled.

Alce ran to stand in front of him.

"Wait! What did you need?" he said deviously. "I could probably help!"

Tyrus glared at him. "Do not patronize me! Bayne is the one who did it and I know she is the only one who can remove it!"

Alce looked at him in surprise. "Are you trying to tell me Bayne did this to you?" He shook his head. "I rather doubt..."

"I am not here for your thoughts or opinions so do not trouble me with them!"

Alce didn't seem to hear him as he continued to ramble on.

"Who is it, I wonder?" He took one of his braids and turned it toward his face. Feathering the neatly tapered end across his cheek and smiled. "Tell me who she is. Who's the girl that changed you so drastically?"

"Bayne."

Alce rolled his eyes. "That's not what I meant."

"It does not matter what you meant. I am leaving."

Alce continued to bar his way. "No, you are not."

Tyrus took a deep breath and released it slowly. "Alce, I am glad that after all these years to find you healthy and sane, but that can change quickly," he threatened.

Alce stifled his laughter as he looked from Tyrus to Evergreen, who shook her head.

"That's very doubtful, dog. You should know that I'm no longer the Alce you remember." His eyes quickly changed from blue to red. "I would be more than happy to give you a well-deserved show of my abilities although you wouldn't be able to return to this girl who seems to have captured your heart," he finished coldly.

Tyrus sighed. He was annoyed yet wary as something besides the odd changing of Alce's eyes made his fur rise. He looked at Alce long and hard as he hovered in front of him, a strange smile on his face.

"C'mon, Tyrus. Tell me. Tell me and I'll make it worth whatever embarrassment you think you're suffering now."

"Tirin."

Alce choked.

Tyrus sat there and watched as the supposed young mage's face reddened from swallowing down the wrong pipe. His own curiosity of what exactly Alce had done to himself was distracting. Mages could do magic, but he had never heard of the strange alterations Alce had done to himself. Elves did not tattoo themselves. And none had color changing eyes. Tyrus sighed.

"Are you surprised?" Tyrus asked dryly.

Alce sat down on the steps as he finally got himself together.

"Tirin Desgjin? The human?" He looked at Tyrus for reassurance. "The one your friend, Darec…"

Tyrus glared at him. "I had nothing to do with what Darec did back then." He paused and gaped at Alce. "How do you know--?"

"Matters not" Alce said, waving him quiet. "Does she know how you feel?"

Tyrus sighed and looked away.

"Ahppahrently not." Evergreen frowned

"It's because of your extra body hair, isn't it?" Alce nodded knowingly.

"Yes." Tyrus laid down, resting his head upon his paws. "But now there is no…"

"Don't bother giving up now, dog," Alce said, irritated.

"What?"

Alce shook his head as he got up.

"Tirin's not one to be told who she can and can't love. She was strong when I last saw her. I'm quite sure she didn't become a pushover as the years increased." He dusted himself off. "She wouldn't care about your so-called curse at all if she cared about you as much as you care for her."

The dog swallowed his words and felt slightly ashamed of himself. As long as he'd lived with her, one would think he of all people would know her better.

"Besides, Bayne didn't curse you…she wouldn't." He watched as Tyrus cocked his head at him. "Her mother could but she's been dead approximately forty years before your visit here."

"Lies." Tyrus shook his head.

Alce glared at him.

"I care not for your thoughts, Alce. I know what the truth is. You cannot tell me what I already know!" Tyrus barked. "Bayne did this to me! She said she would and it happened! I remember--"

Alce grabbed him by his throat and lifted him up from the ground before Tyrus realized what was going on. When he finally grasped his predicament, Alce waved his other hand and Tyrus felt his muscles freeze.

"Alth…"

"You will learn now to never doubt my words!" Alce snapped. "For far too long I've promised to get back at you and Darec for what you put Tirin and me through. To punish all of you for the ridicule and for treating me like I was just so much dirt."

"Ughnn…"

"For the past few minutes I have refrained from taking out my past rage on you only because you seemed to be suffering enough, but for you to even try and put me back in the role of the hapless weakling I used to be is beyond…"

Evergreen reached over and put her hand on his shoulder gently. He looked at her then back at Tyrus, who quickly fell from the air.

They watched as Alce paced the porch, his heavy footfalls causing the rotting wood to vibrate violently as he tried to calm himself.

"Ahlce…"

Alce whirled about, his hands sending forward a strange wave of energy flying out into the swamp. Tyrus watched as five trees were uprooted and sent flying. Evergreen grabbed his arm.

"Ahlce!"

He jerked away. "Don't worry, they were just trees."

Tyrus remained where he landed, remembering how he had hung the young mage upside down in a tree until he passed out. He wouldn't be doing that anytime soon. He cleared his throat.

"I apologize," Tyrus said quietly.

Alce looked at him, his eyes going through a range of colors. He stood there, his fists balled tightly.

Tyrus cleared his throat again as he sat up, trying to look as if he wasn't fazed by the small show of destruction.

"I did not mean to insult you. It is just that I came all this way…"

"Shut. Up." Alce covered his face and stood that way for a long moment, then started to laugh.

"I can't believe I let you get to me like that," he said, chortling.

Tyrus remained quiet.

Alce knelt in front of his company, his smile wide.

"Bayne did not curse you. Despite what you remember or saw or heard. She couldn't have even if she'd wanted to. Her abilities deal with nature. She's a terra-witch and besides, she is partial to children. She wouldn't be able to bring herself to curse a child even if she could, regardless of whatever they did to deserve it."

Evergreen chuckled. "Ahlthough she prahbahbly wishes she cood curse you ah couple ahf times ovah. You were ah terrah."

Alce grinned at her. "Shh! Keep that to yourself." They laughed for a minute, obviously remembering a few things he had done. Tyrus sat quietly, his own anger reluctantly bottled up, as he knew who was responsible for his condition. Their laughter tapered off as Evergreen motioned for Alce to pay attention to their visitor.

"I can see you still don't believe that." Alce sighed and sat down on the porch again. "I'm going to tell you a story and afterwards you're going to tell me about Tirin and yourself. Okay?"

"Yes," Tyrus said wearily.

Evergreen sat down next to Alce as he took a deep breath.

"Approximately forty years ago Bayne and her younger sister lived in Teireyl Valley with their mother. They ran a sort of inn and supply store for travelers pasting between Kelica and Batima. One day they got a very important visitor. The king of Maleatia and a few of his guards stopped in on their way home from Kelica. They had been celebrating quite a bit so the king himself was more than drunk. Night fell and the king found himself attracted to Bayne's mother, so he took advantage of her and threatened to kill her daughters if she said anything. The next morning the king and his lackeys bought more supplies and headed on."

"Bayne's sister knew something was wrong and urged Bayne to ask. All day they pestered her about it until their mother broke down and told them what happened. According to Bayne, her little sister went into a rage none had ever seen, as she had always been the quiet one. Now, at that time, it hadn't been long since their father died and their mother vowed to never use magyk again, as she couldn't save her husband. Bayne hadn't been as adept in her use of magyk and her little sister was, frighteningly so. They calmed her down and eventually thought the matter was settled, after a few days passed and Bayne's sister seemed to have reverted to her reclusive habits. They soon found out that she had been planning a way to get back at the king. They found this out when they discovered her bed empty one morning."

"Bayne's sister went to Maleatia and forcefully made her way into the castle. She confronted the king in front of his queen and cursed him, making it so that any woman bearing his child would die. His queen died painfully within the next few days and distraught, he ordered his guards to bring back the witch who had done this. When Bayne's sister finally returned home, she found that her own mother was dying. She told Bayne what she'd done and Bayne forced her to leave when their mother finally passed. Bayne knew the king would be sending someone after her knowing who she was and where she came from, so set up her own spell upon the ground, a fatal loyalty spell. Teireyl Valley soon turned into what we know as Noir's Swamp as those loyal to that king became some of the trees you see now."

Tyrus scratched his head vigorously, dreading the return home. Regardless of the outcome here, Tirin would surely drench him in that so-called flea solution before allowing him back in the house. He shuddered at the thought. He looked at Alce, who seemed to be waiting for a reaction from the witch's history. Tyrus scratched again.

"So what are you trying to tell me?"

Alce's smile dropped. "I'm trying to tell you that your curse is not a curse, you flea bag!"

Tyrus found himself actually hurt by this barb. "Then what is it and why did it start after she said she would be the one to do it?"

The young wizard smiled again. "Coincidence."

"Doubtful," Tyrus mumbled, scratching again. He paused mid-scratch as Alce's eyes changed to amber.

"I'll prove it." Alce was grinning like a madman as he grabbed Tyrus by the scruff of his neck.

"WHAT ARE YOU DOING?" Tyrus yelped. He tried to pull away only to become paralyzed. He was getting very tired of that spell.

"I need blood."

Tyrus' eyes widened.

CHAPTER NINE

Hunting trip

A week ago, Dale Thessidel had woken up excited about the hunting trip he, his cousin, and his friends had planned for months. It had started out all well and good and then the storm hit on the fourth day of their trip. Then their camp got raided, twice. Then after a day of no game whatsoever, they excitedly and blindly followed a deer into the forest of guardians, where they wandered for three days before realizing where they were.

"This will be funny to us in several years." Dale sighed as the sun went down, leaving them in the darkness of the elven forest once again.

"Funny?" Malik, Dale's younger cousin, scoffed. "You really think so?"

"Yes, think about it." Dale turned on his horse, flinching a bit at how disgusting he felt. He hadn't had a bath in days now. He could feel the layers of filth on his skin cracking and flaking off. His usually neat and tapered beard had grown like a bush. It was driving him mad because it was itching like it was full of ants. "Too many bad things have happened here, but none of it is life-thre--"

Freed, Dale's best friend, laughed feebly from behind the brothers, Borim and Deland. "Dale. Shut up," he groaned. "The only way we could possibly find this funny is if something worse than this trip happens."

With a sigh, all Dale could do was nod in agreement and the earlier moody silence resumed. For another four hours they wandered through the dark forest, their minds working on maybes and what-ifs until Deland's brother, sound asleep, fell from his horse and hit the ground.

The night was interrupted by the burst of genuine laughter when Borim sat up, confused and embarrassed.

"That's our cue to camp," Dale sniggered before dismounting.

"Should we risk a fire?" Malik asked, hopeful that his cousin would say yes. Dale looked at the brothers and then at Freed, then nodded.

"Okay, not that it matters now." Dale pulled his bedding off his horse and before it hit the ground properly he was stretched atop it.

"Why do you say that?" Freed yawned.

Dale turned over to stare up through the trees. "Well, I'm more than sure that the Ao'lean elves know we're here." He yawned. "And apparently we're too pitiful to be concerned with."

Borim laughed. "That's fine with me, I don't need any excitement right--"

A female scream cut through the night, not far from their camp.

"--now," Borim finished.

They were remounted in seconds, riding hard in the direction of the scream.

"Ready, Malik!" Dale ordered over his shoulder before focusing his sharp eyes for the trouble ahead.

"Ready!" Malik whipped his bow out and readied an arrow for flight.

"Do you see her, Dale?" Freed yelled.

"I see our damsel in distress! Straight ahead!" Dale made a sound of surprise. "She's human!"

"Spotted!" Malik said. "Down!" He fired his arrow over the backs of his cousin and Freed.

They all watched as the rider of the black horse was propelled out of his saddle and landed hard on the ground near the unconscious girl. The horse, spooked by its master's sudden dismount, headed back where it came from.

Freed reached for his weapon as the elf made for his own only to discover that he was unarmed. The elven male's eyes darted between them as they surrounded him and the unconscious girl.

"You were right, Dale. She is human." Freed laughed, still amazed by his friend's acute sight.

The elven male looked at the speaker. Freed's strawberry-blonde hair was pulled back, revealing a scruffy face marred and cut from their long visit in the forest of guardians. He was quite sure he looked a sight. Nothing like a noble and more like a ruffian.

"He can more than likely lead us out of this forsaken forest," Freed suggested.

The elf watched the brothers, apparently noting the girl's similar complexion, dismount and start toward him. He retreated, tripping over her.

Malik glared at him. "Can we kill'im after we're finished with'im? For attacking the girl, of course."

Dale looked at Malik, a strange grin on his face. "Why is my little cousin so blood-thirsty? No, Malik, we'll let him go. Don't want to start a war for killing an elf who looked to be a noble of some sort."

The elf watched them for a moment more before he started screaming.

"*Aleur! Aleur, yond'lo mah! Yond'lo...ughn*!" Borim hit the elf in his stomach and knocked him down.

"Dale, do you have rope so we can..."

The sound of more hooves coming their way caused Malik to jump down and retrieve the girl. The elf yelled at them only to be hit across the face before the five hunters took off.

They rode straight for about ten minutes and suddenly found themselves out of the forest with no problem. The girl remained unconscious in Malik's arms as they continued toward the Vale.

"Something's off about that," Freed called ahead to Dale.

Dale shrugged. "Let's deal with that when we are in more familiar country," he yelled back.

Night brought with it a silence that made the Great Hall seem like it was frozen in time. Shining brightly through the stained-glass windows, the moon painted the Great Hall with a myriad of colors, giving it an almost ethereal feel as the glass figures were projected eerily throughout the room like colorful ghosts.

Angry voices echoed through the passageways before arriving at the main door to the Great Hall. The silence was broken when the owners of the voices entered. The moonlight images of past High Lords were chased away when light filled the ornate Hall.

Daynel crept closer to the Hall as light flared from beneath the service entrance. She had no concern for being caught because all the servants had been sent home. She listened to the heavy footsteps as the group of men made their way to the far end of the room.

"And...her leave?" Baelor snarled.

Daynel frowned, wishing she could have heard the whole sentence. The only immediate solution was to open the door. She swallowed and grasped the doorknob. She took a deep breath and closed her eyes. Painstakingly she turned the doorknob, slowly and gently, trying to reduce any possible sound. A soft click and the inability to turn the knob anymore told her that half the job was done. Now all she had to do was open the door.

"…and after the Young Lord took off through the gate, we followed procedures before chasing after him." Rane explained. "Upon reachin' a certain point in the forest we…uh…heard Lady Tirin scream and a few paces closer we came upon the Young Lord's horse, riderless."

"And then?" Baelor urged impatiently. He was furious at them for letting her get away, but also with himself for his behavior. He glared at Lord Deimiyon, thinking about the High Lord's son. This only made him angrier.

Rane looked at Zeph, who quickly took up the report.

"We backtracked the horse's path to find the Young Lord semiconscious and wounded with the humans riding off into the distance. Dain, Merca, Lor, and Irid took chase after them, but due to their lead lost them in the darkness. The Young Lord came to enough to inform us that the humans had taken Lady Tirin."

"They caught me off guard," Darec said from behind, entering from another door.

"Son!" Lord Deimiyon exclaimed in surprise. "You should be resting."

"I was shot in the arm, not a lung, father." Darec looked away from his father, annoyed. "I'm fine."

"Still, you should be…"

Darec groaned. "I can't rest while Tirin is still in the hands of those brutes!"

Baelor scoffed. Curious, Darec eyed the older elf.

"Sire?"

"You realize you all but put her in the danger she's in now?" Baelor kept his eyes on the boy's face.

Darec glared. "What?"

"Excuse me?" The High Lord stood straight, his confusion obvious. "What does that mean, Baelor?"

Sire Baelor sat down at the great meeting table, putting space between himself and the Young Lord. "Your boy here interfered in matters that had nothing, NOTHING, to do with him!" he growled.

Darec drew closer to the table, irritated. "You weren't going to tell her!" he yelled.

His father covered his face and shook his head. "Darec, please don't tell me you were eavesdropping again. Don't tell me you did what I think you've done." The High Lord turned and headed toward the Lord's chair, his tired footsteps muffled as they reached the rich mauve carpet leading up to the dais.

"Father! He wasn't going to tell her!"

"That wasn't your business!" both Baelor and Deimiyon shouted back.

Daynel watched the five men become deathly quiet. Darec tensed and balled his fists, the tell-tale sign of his anger.

"Darec," Lord Deimiyon said calmly. "What exactly is your involvement in this? Tell me what happened."

"Unlike someone here, I was trying to show her how much she was needed."

"Boy…" Baelor started, falling silent when the High Lord shook his head.

Darec continued. "She said that you didn't want anything to do with her anymore." Darec wanted to smile as the look on Baelor's face melted into obvious shame. "I…" He paused, unsure whether to keep his next words to himself. Darec took a deep breath. "I asked her to be my wife."

"You did what?" the other four men exclaimed in unison.

Daynel fell back from the door, sure that her heart had just exploded.

"You did what, boy?"

Darec almost smirked at Baelor as the older elf stood on the other side of the table. "Stop calling me 'Boy'. Please. Sire."

Sire Baelor stared at Darec in disbelief. "You asked my daughter to marry you?"

Darec nodded, almost too proudly.

"And being my daughter, she turned you down." Baelor's mouth held a sly smirk before he sat back down, watching Darec's arrogant posture falter.

"She didn't give herself time to consider my offer…she was too upset that her *biological* father told her to get out of his life."

"*I did not tell her that*!" Baelor shot up out of his seat again, his fist slamming resoundingly on the hardwood table. The guards started for him only to pause in their advance as Baelor glared daringly at them.

"Darec," High Lord Deimiyon warned. "Do not do that again."

The arrogant look Darec gave Sire Baelor lingered just long enough to make him hate the Young Lord. With a slight smile playing on his lips, the Young Lord turned away from Baelor before starting again.

"I followed her through the city, saw her sail over the gate and chased after her once these fools got themselves together enough to open the gates for me." He grinned regardless of the situation. "Her use of magyk was very impressive." He looked at Tirin's father expecting some kind of acknowledgment but received none. "I caught up with her only because she seemed to have had some type of accident, but I was unable to convince her to come back."

Darec paused for the briefest moment and Baelor watched a strange look flutter across the boy's face, telling him that there was more to the story than he was telling. Something he didn't want to share.

The Young Lord continued. "I was going to take her to the edge of the forest. It wasn't long after that …that the humans showed up." He massaged his wounded arm absently.

"You should have brought her back—" Sire Baelor started.

"She wouldn't have it," Darec insisted. "She's too much like her father."

Baelor does laugh, genuinely this time. "That means she did say 'no' to your proposal."

Daynel almost smirked, but it wasn't enough to withstand the disgust she was feeling for the man she was so in love with. For years she'd been in love with Darec, and for years he'd ignored her obvious attempts to show him. It wasn't fair how life was treating her. She hated Tirin when he hated her, teased her relentlessly to appease him when he let her join in. She supported all his schemes and plots and still his eyes only saw Tirin. Then, when his feelings changed for the human, Daynel couldn't help but hate Tirin more. Daynel became invisible to him, while Tirin had the Young Lord's heart and didn't even know it.

"Is it interesting, brat?" a voice said behind her.

She jumped, a scream ready to tear free, but was able to stifle it painfully by biting her tongue.

Daynel wiped the tears away and finally saw the three behind her. She hadn't heard a sound of their approach. Tyrus stood there, more menacing than ever, joined by two others. There was a strange blonde elf whose face was awfully familiar, and a tall cloaked female who remained near the back of the room. The surprise was short-lived when it finally hit that the weird blonde had called her a brat.

"What?" She straightened up to face them. "How dare you--"

Tyrus stepped forward and watched the redhead stumble back. "Why are you out here?"

Daynel swallowed her apprehension. Tyrus was not one she had gotten close to while they grew up. He had been Darec's right-hand and something had always made her uneasy around him even before he was cursed. But she wasn't going to let him intimidate her too much.

"None of your business," she hissed. Inside she wanted to curl up. He was so creepy! His unruly dark hair shadowed most of his face yet did nothing to veil those intense eyes. He stared at her with that emotionless face of his.

Alce grinned to the cloaked person, who immediately started forward, shaking her head.

"Well, then, brat, let's go in, shall we?" He grabbed Daynel's arm and dragged her toward the door. Alce smiled broadly when she tried to pull away from him. He shoved the door open and proudly walked in with Daynel fighting him all the way, unconcerned with the sudden alarmed looks from the men inside the Hall.

"Greeting men of Ao'lean!" Alce called happily. "We found this one nosing about outside, so we figured there was something interesting going on in here."

The two guards, Rane and Zeph, Sire Baelor, Darec, and the High Lord turned fully to watch as the blonde elf half dragged Daynel into the room accompanied by the dark cloaked elf.

"Tyrus! Where have you been?" Baelor exclaimed.

Tyrus watched the older elf for a moment then answered. "I had something to do." He looked at the faces of the five men in the room before him. "There are guards at the house, Sire. What is happening?"

Baelor took a deep breath and sat down again. "Tirin's been taken."

"What?"

Alce pouted noisily. "And here I was ready to see her again." He shrugged, shoving Daynel away from him. "Ah well, let's go get her."

High Lord Deimiyon stared at him for a moment before motioning toward him. "Who are you?"

From their surprised reaction, Tyrus could only guess that Alce's eyes did their weird trick. "This is Alce Deland."

"Alce?" Darec laughed almost uncontrollably before realizing no one saw the joke he was seeing.

"I see you haven't changed, still the ass you always were." Alce gave a false smile.

High Lord Deimiyon raised a brow at him. "If you remember him, then you know you are to give him the respect of his--"

"You can't give what you don't have, and there's no chance of even a little." Alce shook his head reproachfully. "I'm sorry." He faced Baelor, sporting violet eyes a shade or two darker than Tyrus'. "You *are* getting a group together to go and get her? Right?"

"Ahlce, ifen Bayne returned..." the cloaked figure started, surprising the others, who had forgotten she was there. Alce waved her quiet.

"No one's gonna bother that place. Besides she hasn't bothered to call on us in two years. A bit of adventure won't hurt. Anyway, this won't take long."

Darec's attention was piqued by the old woman's name. "Bayne?" He looked at Tyrus, realizing he must have gone to face the old woman again, to get her to do something about his curse. Now the only question was, why now?

"You are wondering about Tyrus' business, Darec." The Alce smirked.

"What is it to you?" Darec snapped, not appreciating being called out like that.

Tyrus watched Baelor and noted how suddenly he looked so much older. There was more to this situation. "We are wasting time."

"Agreed," Deimiyon called, pulling his eyes from the cloaked woman. "The group will be those in this room, save myself."

"What?" Daynel screeched. "I don't want to go!"

"Next time don't become concerned with what does not concern you." Deimiyon gave her a withering glare. "Baelor, you have free reign on whatever you think you will need."

"Thank you, Deimiyon." He looked at the Young Lord for a moment. "You sure you weren't hurting her in some way?"

Darec froze. "Why in the world are you asking that?" he exclaimed. "I was trying to save her!"

"Calm down." Tyrus looked at him coldly.

A momentary look of apprehension fluttered across Darec's face before vanishing. "You are still blaming me for this?"

"I'm just asking a question, Young Lord. Something had to make those humans think she needed rescuing."

"Rescuing?"

"Rane, how long were the humans in the forest?"

"I believe five days, Sire," the younger guard answered immediately.

"So they didn't know where they were for a while."

"No, sire. Just a bunch of hapless hunters."

"What has that to do with anything?" Darec rolled his eyes impatiently.

Baelor shook his head at the Young Lord. "They shot you once--"

"I'm quite sure they would have shot me again."

"But if they just wanted to take her, you would be dead. Something made them think she needed to be rescued. If it were otherwise, they wouldn't have been run off by just four guards."

Darec considered his options. "She was hurt."

"Hurt?" Baelor watched his face. "Hurt how?"

Evergreen nudged Alce, motioning toward Tyrus as this new information was revealed. They watched as everything about Tyrus said calm except the surprising lengthening of his black claws. Tyrus flexed his hands and realized something was wrong with them. After a quick glance, he hid them beneath his cloak. He looked to see if anyone else noticed and locked eyes with a grinning Alce.

"Calm down, Sire," Darec grumbled. "The spell she used to get over the gate…I think she lost control of it. Her magyk is impressive but it's not very strong just yet. I'm guessing it gave out. When I caught up with her she was holding her side and was rather dirty. She must have taken a serious tumble."

The High Lord nodded, rubbing his chin. "So…"

"She looked abused," Baelor concluded. "And with you chasing after her they could only make one assumption."

Darec wanted to smile.

"So you think they'll treat her badly when they find out?"

Baelor's tired face suddenly became even wearier. "If they are anything like elves…yes, they will."

Tyrus gave a confused look to Sire Baelor. "Is there something I am missing?"

Darec watched as the older elf pulled Tyrus further from the rest of them. Minutes passed and the Young Lord observed the two, waiting to see the expression on the dog-boy's face when he found out that Tirin was half elf.

Then Tyrus looked up. It wasn't what Darec was expecting. Immediately he knew it wasn't Tirin's blood causing the look he was receiving.

Baelor's sour expression held no candle to the hateful look on Tyrus' face.

This was going to be a very interesting trip.

CHAPTER TEN

<u>*Pet*</u>

It would be another hour before the sun rose. The castle was dark and still asleep. Despite everything that had happened earlier, only one found it hard to sleep.

Tyrus wandered the grounds absently, his mind still trying to cope with what he'd learned. She was half elf! It had been a thought he entertained off and on concerning her ability to even live here in Ao'lean, but he could not quite believe it now that it was true. How was it that Baelor couldn't figure that out?

Slowly he made his way into the garden at the rear of the palace. High Lord Deimiyon had insisted they rest in the guest quarters. That silenced Daynel's constant whining. His pace slowed as he followed the winding paths. Even the flowers seemed to be asleep as their heads were tightly shut, waiting for the sun. He walked over to a small circle of softly glowing white flowers, caphony flowers, Tirin's favorite. Their scent was strong even while closed. She'd been gone not even a day and he felt like his heart had been wrenched from his chest. The idea that she was mistakenly kidnapped seemed too ridiculous to consider despite the facts. She would be found and brought back to where she belonged…with him.

Tyrus looked up at the sky, its inky darkness lightening on the very edge of the horizon.

He wasn't cursed. That was what he wanted to tell her when he returned.

It wasn't a curse, but his heritage.

His father's bloodline was the cause of this. It was a talent passed through the males of his family, skipping a generation or two every now and then.

How Alce was able to tell all that from a little bit of (reluctantly given) blood was beyond Tyrus' understanding. Alce made the attempt to explain, but he quickly saw that his excitement over the 'science' of it was not shared.

With Tirin's help it became more than just a bloodline ability. His father would have been able to tell him about it when he was younger if he had been able to return from the same mission that Baelor had lost his arm to.

Tyrus slowly made his way through the courtyard, his eyes unconsciously scanning ahead of him. Flickering torch light in the stable area made him pause for a second.

Who else could possibly be up?

The scent of Thesimier surprised him as he made his way over to the stables. Tirin's horse was a shy, smoke gray mare that usually refused to leave the property. Did she sense her mistress' trouble? Tyrus paused at the opening and sighed when he saw Sire Baelor standing there talking softly to the horse.

Thesimier was lightly loaded with bags of what looked to be clothing.

The older elf must have been unable to sleep and in his unease, must have gone to retrieve Tirin's horse.

"She'll want these," Baelor mumbled to himself before folding several items and adding them to the bags. The look on Baelor's face caused Tyrus to feel guilty. Had he just stayed at the

Comne he would have been able to prevent whatever had happened, and Tirin would still be here, safe.

Tyrus looked at his black nails. But then he would have never known that he no longer had to restrain his emotions, that his change was controllable, that he no longer had to hold himself back from expressing his true feeling. Not to Tirin…and definitely not to Darec. Now that she apparently remembered what had happened, she would not question his attitude toward the brat prince.

"Where were you?"

Tyrus looked up to find Baelor standing in front of him, the look on his face blank. His eyes were weary and circled with the lack of sleep.

Guilt hit him hard as words refused to come quick enough. He found himself back in the Inner garden, approaching Darec and Tirin and seeing them kiss. Anger replaced his guilt easily. She remembered what Darec had done; why had she kissed him?

Sire Baelor watched the younger elf's face. What seemed to be concern slowly changed to something else.

"Tyrus?"

"I am sorry for not being there for her, Sire."

Baelor moved closer to the boy. "But what called you away?"

Tyrus' violet eyes grew dark. "Anger." He quickly walked off, back toward the sleeping quarters. The sun was threatening over the horizon.

*****

The day after their so called rescue of the 'maiden', their luck took a turn for the worst. Fog blinded their return trek and the brothers; Borim and Deland, got separated from the rest of them. A pair of starved worgs decided then to hunt them when the party attempted to search for the brothers. They were further separated when it was realized where their blind trek had led them. The Goblin's woods.

And then the girl, Tirin, was suddenly able to speak human when it had already been established that she could only speak elven.

That was when the goblins attacked.

A day later found Malik and Tirin in the small human kingdom of Kiten. They were grubby, filthy, exhausted, and as far as they knew, the only survivors of Dale's small hunting party. Malik decided then to be rid of the girl they rescued and be done with whatever evil she brought with her.

*****

Randoll Norsmon had been on duty that day and watched as the two approached. He remembered how the boy, Malik, had dragged the poor girl into the gateway of the castle. Oh, how irritated he had been.

The boy, Malik didn't want to have anything to do with her, but leaving her in the wild would have disappointed his deceased cousin so he'd brought her here. Both of them had come in looking like wild animals, but she was in worse shape due to the restraints he said were necessary. Malik had tied and gagged her with a material that caused a fever-inducing rash. The poor girl was rambling incoherently, but Malik didn't care. The boy said it was to keep her from casting any demonic spells, given that she was half elf. This bit of information was mentioned with impeccable timing, uttered as Prince Sayer came out to see to the commotion in front of his home. Elves were a subject the Prince was enthralled with, for the moment. Therefore, without question the prince took the girl in.

That was four days ago. The prince had anxiously waited for this day since the girl's arrival. A visitor was expected at any moment, one that was maybe stranger than the girl. Prince Sayer couldn't wait to show her off.

From the corner of his eye, Randoll watched the visitor approach the gate. For the longest time Randoll had suspected this man of being something he said he wasn't. He couldn't put his finger on it, but something about Master Gar seemed…artificial.

Randoll's job consisted of watching people, remembering details. This man, Gar, just seemed too perfect. He was beautiful, like a woman, with a delicate, graceful way about him, yet there was no way to mistake his masculinity.

Randoll coughed. He would never say that aloud. He was a guard for his majesty, not a judge on who was manly and who was not. But Master Gar could not be ignored. He had bright, clear blue eyes that became icy when he was annoyed, and he was always annoyed. His blonde hair was more like spun gold than spun gold. A chiseled face was somehow soft in its features and the perfect alabaster skin would spark a jealous rage in even a woman of the most delicate nature. He was not a man of brawn, but one would think twice before trying him. Randoll watched as Master Gar passed him without so much as a smile or nod. As usual. The man was secretive, only speaking with Prince Sayer. No one knew how old he was, where he came from, or what he did in that room that all but Master Gar and his Majesty were forbidden to enter. Master Gar disappeared into the main courtyard and Randoll quickly returned to his job.

Gar practically floated down the hallway, his thoughts consuming him as he passed people without realizing they were there. He was far from concerned with the ways of humans. He slowed his pace, fed up with the likes of any race that found it a natural pastime to gossip. He knew what was thought of him, how they felt when he passed them or even looked at him. He heard the petrified whispers of the servants and the guards. Their fear was well deserved and wanted. No, it was rare for a human to possess the gift of magyk and still be sane. He had heard it all. That he had traded his soul or that he had none to start with. Gar almost smiled. He would have given his eyeteeth to see the reaction of them all if they were to ever find out the truth.

"Master Gar!"

Gar stood straight, his disgust with the young prince almost beyond toleration, but he was able to contain it. This was the only person who had the audacity to think himself equal to him. He turned to face the young prince.

Prince Sayer was a tall, well-built human male with smiling steel-blue eyes that easily hid the intent of their owner. He had the face of a boy, encircled by curly, ink-black hair cut short to retain that 'innocent' look of a child. He was still a boy by elven standards, but far from it in humans, as in less than a year Prince Sayer would become king.

"Yes, Prince Sayer."

"Come with me. I have something to show you." Quickly the Prince led the way down one of many hallways. "A boy brought me this girl--"

"What you do with her is your own business, your majesty," Gar grumbled.

"She's delightfully savage, this girl," Prince Sayer continued cheerfully, ignoring his remark. "She's been here for nearly a week now and still has the desire to fight."

Gar remained indifferent as he followed the young monarch. "And this makes her interesting?"

Prince Sayer looked at him, rather hurt. "Master Gar, I would think that you would be a little interested." He rubbed his hands together as he stopped. "I think you will be anyway, being that she was rescued from Ao'lean."

"What?" Gar asked in startled confusion, shocked by the mere mention of the great elven city. "Explain yourself."

Prince Sayer sighed. "My excitement mostly stems from your reaction when you see her, hear her." He smiled broadly as he began walking again. "She is an enigma, one that promises hours of entertainment."

"If you say so." He rolled his eyes. "But can you make this quick? I have things to do."

The two walked down a series of corridors, passageways, and stairs. Finally they reached the dungeon area.

"I made a point for no one to come down this way save for one guard." He grinned at Gar, impressed with himself. "The women here are such gossips and the men are superstitious. They're about as scared of her as they are of you."

"Really?" Gar jeered.

"Here we are." Prince Sayer knocked on the door then put his ear to it and smiled.

Not a sound came from inside.

"Tirin?"

Gar raised an eyebrow in surprise. "You've named her already?"

"No, no, the boy that brought her here said that was her name." Prince Sayer knocked on the door again then opened the small window located at eye level. "Tirin, love, you have com--"

"Stop using my name, you animal!" Her voice was sharp with insult and thick with an accent Gar never thought he would hear again.

"The boy had said that she couldn't speak human but he was apparently deceived. He also said she could do magyk...or something to that effect. Said she's half elf."

"Half elf...are you sure?" Gar peered into the small room, now interested. Elves were very selective about who they associated with, if anyone, race-wise. All the major elven cities were isolated from other towns of mixed races, all surrounded by walls and solely inhabited by elves. But for one to have mated with someone not elven was rare. Sayer nodded then retold the story of how the boy, Malik, and his friends came upon her.

Inside, the slight movement of chains was heard. Through the dimness he could see her. Dressed in an old maid's uniform that was maybe four sizes too big for her, she looked malnourished as the shoulders threatened to slide off of her petite frame.

Gar's satchel suddenly began to move. He quickly pulled back, trying to hide it from the Prince.

"Isn't she neat?" Sayer rubbed his hairless chin. "I wonder if her parents were in love or if it was a violent conception."

Gar gave him a disgusted look. "What does that matter?"

He grinned. "It doesn't." He shrugged. "I took the liberty of using that sipher you gave me. To keep her from casting any unnecessary spells." The prince smiled arrogantly as Gar raised an eyebrow, amused that the Prince thought him impressed with his use of an item he created simply to shut him up. The sipher did nothing. Purely ornamental. But the useless runes and glyphs Gar painted across its brass surface made it look impressive.

The Prince turned and headed back down the hallway. What he was up to was anyone's guess. As soon as the prince was gone, Gar opened his satchel. His compendium was agitated and the girl had something to do with it.

He watched as the pages fluttered rapidly back and forth before stopping on an old spell he hadn't worked on in years. The spell was missing only one major component: a dragon's soul, an ingredient that was hard to come by because either dragons were no longer part of this world or because they had gone into their hundred-year slumber. Gar peeked through the small window and almost smiled as she stood there staring back at him. Part of him wanted to burst into laughter right then and there. If the girl had any magykal abilities, and his book implied that she did, she would know that the sipher was a fake. He had created it to shut the prince up. But then that would mean that the girl knew about the sipher and he doubted the prince had told her about it.

"Why am I so interest?" Tirin snapped.

"*Interesting*, child." He watched her turn her back to him. "You cast a spell near the goblin's territory. They're attracted to magyk. They didn't teach you that in school?" The last he spoke in Elvish.

Tirin whirled around to face him. The light of the torches filtered into her cell somewhat, illuminating her dirty brown face and revealing the childish pout that he found surprisingly endearing.

"Oh, I have many surprises, but that's for another time."

"Whatever." Her look of surprise faded quickly before she headed back into the darkness of her dungeon.

"Don't shrug me off just yet, lady. There are things about you that are intriguing, and Prince Sayer has his ways of getting the information he wants."

All he received for his warning was the tinkling of her chains.

"Tirin?" Gar pulled back as a growl floated out of the darkness. The timbre of her growl was very feral. Maybe too feral. "Are you really half elf and not half ...animal?"

Tirin actually wanted to laugh at him, but a small part of her entertained the idea that it could be possible. She had noticed the changes in herself every now and then. She looked at the strange blonde man from her dark corner. He couldn't see her, but she could see him clearly. She could also hear the hesitant steps of someone else heading down the hall behind him. She could smell the alcohol on this new person's breath. How many times had she shrugged off the idea that when she first forced Tyrus to revert that she had taken part of him and incorporated it into herself?

"Tirin?"

She hugged herself tightly. She would have time to think it through now.

Gar stopped talking. She wasn't listening to a word he was saying anyway and he didn't blame her. He hated to agree with the brat Prince, but she was definitely interesting. Memories filled his head as he peered into the dark cell, her eyes reflecting the torchlight like a cat's. A human who may or may not be half elf, she definitely spoke like she belonged there. She was probably scared. That could be the only reason she didn't use magyk to get herself out. Not knowing where she was, using her abilities to get out of here would more than likely put her into more danger than she could handle. Gar looked at his book again. He had better get to investigating her before Sayer grew tired of her. He turned in time to see the guard the prince had assigned to be her caretaker. He was a sad and depressing old man smelling highly of alcohol.

CHAPTER ELEVEN

Camp

They had been traveling for more than two weeks, and had found no indication of where to find the human hunting party or Tirin.

"This is ridiculous!" Daynel whined. "Why am I here?"

The small parade of elves made their way through unfamiliar territory, cloaked to hide their race and quiet so they wouldn't attract much attention when on main roads.

"You can always return home, brat," Alce snapped, no longer amused by her discomfort. The redhead glowered at the blonde.

"Stop calling me that."

"Stop acting like one."

"Both of you shut up," Tyrus growled from between them.

Baelor smiled slightly as the boy sprinted ahead of the group. This was a new and improved Tyrus; something had made the boy more confident. Baelor could only think that somehow, Tyrus had gotten control over his curse. He raised an eyebrow. Maybe it wasn't a curse after all? The older elf nodded to himself while watching Tyrus disappear ahead. Tyrus' whole demeanor had changed since returning from wherever he had escaped to; he was more vocal and aggressive. The older elf eyed Alce, for a brief moment seeing the younger version, the shy boy who would come by to see Tirin when she had a bad day. The years had definitely given him some backbone. His father, Master Nicholae Deland, wouldn't recognize his own son. Nevertheless, Baelor was sure that Alce had something to do with the sudden change in Tyrus. The boy was done hiding his feelings and Baelor couldn't help but feel a little proud.

He watched the path ahead sadly, his mind coming back to the venture at hand. They had already searched four towns and come up with nothing. No one knew of, had seen, or heard anything. And Darec wasn't helping the situation. He was arrogant to the point of getting them chased out of one town with his condescending attitude toward humans.

Tyrus observed Sire Baelor, the older elf deep in thought as his face now showed his true age. Their search had so far revealed nothing. Whatever scent there may have been had gone cold days ago. They were just wandering from town to town. An idea suddenly hit him and he made his way back toward the leader of this depressed group.

"Sire."

Baelor looked at him blankly. "Hm?"

"I tire of following Darec. I think I have a better way…something I should have done when we left Ao'lean."

"Really?" Darec snapped, annoyed. "And exactly what makes you think you know best about this? You weren't there, remember?"

The glare in those violet eyes caused Darec to recoil a bit. "Your sarcasm is not necessary, Young Lord." Tyrus snapped back.

"Okay. We're resting here. This is camp." Baelor sighed, feeling like he was babysitting all of a sudden. "It's evident we're all tired."

The party stopped in what seemed to be the center of a thin forest. Several minutes later a warm fire was going and food was simmering.

"Camp would've been set up a lot faster if Tyrus had helped!" Darec complained loudly as he rolled out his bedroll. He frowned a little as Daynel slid her own closer to his.

"That's true. Where did he run off to?" Baelor searched the camp and spied Alce's cloaked companion making her way back to the center of camp with a bundle of clothing in her hand.

"Ah, he's off doing his doggie duties," Daynel quipped and couldn't help but smile as Darec burst into laughter.

A single howl far off in the distance silenced the young Prince's mirth. They all looked toward the direction of the howl.

"Is that--" Zeph started only to pause when the lone howl was joined by dozens of others.

"I want to go home!" Daynel whined.

Alce couldn't help the smile on his face. Apparently, this wasn't normal Tyrus behavior. This adventure may turn out to be more exciting than he thought. "What is he up to, Evergreen?" he asked suddenly.

Baelor looked from the blonde to the cloaked female. She sat next to Alce, not bothering to remove her cloak or lower her cowl. Baelor didn't think she did it to hide herself from them but for their comfort. He didn't care about her heritage, but he couldn't speak for the accompanying guards or for Daynel or Darec.

"E's gooin to try an find hur scent. It seems the redhead's purfuum is ovahpowahring." The tall elf curled up on the sleeping mat that Alce had laid out for her and promptly fell asleep.

Daynel looked humiliated only for a second before regaining her snobbish attitude.

"That can't be helped. I'm a Lady." She fluffed her curls.

Darec frowned. "What makes him think that the 'scent' was lost?"

Alce laughed. "Maybe being that he's the only one that can smell it?" He raised an eyebrow at the Prince. "He would know."

"I don't understand what he's trying to prove," Darec growled. "This was the way they came."

Alce sighed in annoyance. "You were unconscious, how would you know which way they went?"

Darec remained silent as all eyes turned to him. While Baelor removed his boots and rubbed his feet, Darec opened his mouth to retort but was cut off.

"Shut up."

They all looked at the old Imperial. "Since the start of this trek you have done nothing but make finding clues harder."

The expression on Baelor's face did not convey the emotion in his voice, he was so drained.

"I have not!" Darec blustered out.

Baelor continued, ignoring the prince. "It's almost as if you're trying to drag this out with all the trouble you've caused."

Baelor's eyes finally locked onto the Young Lord. "I've been wondering why you were so adamant about us coming east when the nearest human town was northwest. And with my concerns for what torture my daughter could be going through clouding my better judgment, I allowed you to lead this rescue." He glared at Darec. "But Alce is right, you wouldn't have a clue as to where the hunters went. The guards that chased after them when you were found would probably know best and of course Tyrus would be a better guide than you."

Darec's mouth worked soundlessly. Honestly, he didn't care that they were going to turn around. This trek had given more than enough time for the weather and the fauna to erase whatever trail there may have been.

"I--" Darec started only to be cut off by a haunting howl.

The guards were up and armed with Darec following their lead. He groaned as Daynel cowered behind him.

Alce and Evergreen didn't bother to stand up so Baelor didn't either. He figured that the young mage would know best if there was trouble and besides, Evergreen remained fast asleep.

The eerie howl faded, leaving the woods silent.

"There." Alce observed the small gathering with playful green eyes. "Nothing to be afraid of."

"It's nothing," Baelor informed them before stretching out on his mat. "Zeph."

"Yes, Sire."

"You have first watch, I'll take second. Rane, you take third." The two guards nodded at Baelor. The older guard disappeared into the woods while the younger readied the other's sleeping pad.

"That's it?" Daynel squeaked. "Shouldn't both of them be out? I mean we're in the middle of the woods in some strange--"

"Daynel. Tere's nahthing 'ere ta--"

"Silence, Ferine," Darec snapped. He started to say something rude but found himself suddenly upside down. "Hey!"

Daynel scrambled back quickly, looking from Darec to Alce, whose eyes were now a deep red.

"I," Alce said smoothly yet threateningly, remaining seated on his pad, "have no qualms about showing you the respect you so deserve."

"Put me down!" Darec hissed. He looked to his guard, who just stood there watching. "Why aren't you doing anything?"

"Like what?" the young guard asked.

"Alce," Baelor said simply. Alce smirked then dropped the Young Lord onto his pad.

Baelor sighed; he was going to be so happy when this whole ordeal was done.

Darec gave Alce a glare and then gave one to Rane before making himself comfortable on his mat. Darec searched the trees around them. Tyrus was different. Alce had done something to him;

he was now too comfortable as a wolf. He no longer had sway over Tyrus as he had when he was younger. Neither did he have a plan for what to do if they found Tirin alive. She would definitely tell now. He could try and rely on the fact that she was just as prideful as her father and that the secret would remain kept. Too humiliating or damning to bring up. But she was aware that he had thrown her from his horse, her eyes had said as much before she was knocked unconscious. She would make him pay and with Tyrus behind her, she would have no reservations.

Daynel watched her prince secretly from her mat, pretending to do her hair. His eyes were deep in thought. Worry filled them, but not for Tirin. This was a selfish concern. Daynel knew all of Darec's little quirks and tics, and she knew this look well. She suddenly found herself wondering what Tirin was going through. To be 'rescued' by her kidnappers…and what would they do to her when they found out that she wasn't even full human? Daynel recalled what Baelor said back in the throne room about them treating her badly. She felt a twinge of guilt.

"You okay, Lady Daynel?" Rane asked coyly, seeing her fret. She looked at him with wide eyes.

"Yuh-yes." She pulled her blankets over her head.

Rane went back to check the horses once more before bedding down himself. The young guard passed Alce and Evergreen, and Baelor found himself wondering where Alce had been all this time. Why had he run away in the first place without a word to anyone since? Then, he wondered, what exactly brought him back to the world of Ao'lean?

"Sire?" Alce said, smiling. "You were staring."

Baelor returned his smile. "Just wondering--"

"What brings me back to Ao'lean?" Alce finished. He grinned when Baelor nodded.

"That, and what did you do to Tyrus?" he concluded.

Alce's eyes turned a deep calming blue. "Tirin, that's the answer to the first inquiry. And to the latter…well you may have to ask Tyrus that. I don't really think he wants me to explain it."

Baelor nodded. "What about Tirin?"

Alce's eyes went black for a second before turning yellow.

"Tyrus told me about her ability to do magyk and that she received a gift from the Grand Ao'lean." He knew his chameleon eyes had given him away, having no control over what color they displayed. But he hoped his words would distract him from the obvious.

The smirk on the older elf's face told him that he wasn't fooled, but he understood.

"Did he now?" The retired Imperial paused over the answer. "So you knew already?"

"That she's half elf? Well, I was never totally sure, just knew it was possible. Either she was a sign of things to come or you were truly her father and somehow didn't know."

Baelor sighed.

"It's not your fault," Alce assured him.

Baelor shook his head. "But it is. There is no way for it not to be." He sighed again. "I pushed her mother away, gave her no other choice but to leave me. I—"

"You're going to blame yourself for her death now, aren't you?" Alce frowned.

Baelor almost smiled.

"Why am I even telling you this?"

Alce shrugged then started again. "Because. Who better to understand than someone in somewhat the same situation?" Alce looked at the sleeping Ferine behind him. "She may not be human but the reaction would have been the same. The difference is we were isolated, while you were watched all the time."

"Alce."

"I am unable to lie, Sire, you know this already," he informed the older elf quietly. "I can withhold information though." Alce's eyes became a warm brown. "The Alce you remember went through a lot of changes to become the one you see now, changes that wouldn't have occurred had I not left. I'd still be the same fearful boy you remember."

Baelor frowned. "What has that—"

"Tirin's mother loved you and her death was not in vain. Tirin is proof of that."

Unable to find his voice, Baelor remained quiet.

"If you had the chance to go back and fix everything, the result would be the same, just through different circumstances." Alce paused as the look on Baelor's face became lost for a moment. He slowly stood up.

"I—" Baelor started but his voice cracked despite his ability to keep his face void of emotion.

Lowering his eyes, Alce nodded. "No need." He watched the elder elf's feet walk away from him and toward the edge of camp.

"E's gonna ahsk you 'bout—" Evergreen mumbled from her mat.

"I know."

The night passed without interruption and Rane found himself watching Daynel sleep more than the surrounding area. An exhausted shadow slid into camp and curled up quietly near the horses so as not to alarm anyone with his odor.

An hour later the sky brightened with soft hues of rose and amber. Daynel yawned, then quickly covered her mouth, seeing Rane watching her. "Morning."

Rane blushed and nodded at her before getting up to make one last circuit of the perimeter.

Baelor knew if circumstances were different, he would find himself meddling, but now he couldn't care less. He looked at the mat besides his; it was as neat as when he first laid it out, and he wondered if Tyrus was okay.

Her shrill scream woke everyone up.

Rane bounded over Darec to get to Daynel quickly and was thrown back as she crashed into him.

"It moved! It! Moved!" She blindly pointed behind her toward the horses. She'd draped blankets over them to shield her changing into fresher clothing.

"What?" Darec yawned, mildly amused. "What has freaked you out now?"

A large mound of black fur sat less than four feet away from where she was dressing. Zeph and Rane stared at it. Darec raised an eyebrow.

"Poke it."

The mound moved, revealing a tail and a glowing armlet. "'Poke me and lose that arm."

The guards backed off while Tyrus uncurled and stood on wobbly feet. "Cannot sleep with you hovering above me!" he snapped.

Alce snickered as the party backed away.

"Well?" Darec asked. "Find anything?"

Baelor finished repacking and cleared his throat. "Tyrus, please. Do you have any news?"

The wolf shook vigorously, dislodging sticks and leaves. "We're heading the wrong way."

CHAPTER TWELVE

Close

It had been almost a month and there had been no word of anyone searching for the dolled-up pet of Prince Sayer's. Gar wondered what went through her mind as she stared restlessly from the balcony of his private chambers.

The garden below called to her with its varying array of flowery perfumes and bird songs, flaunting a freedom she had more than likely taken for granted when she was home. She was dressed in a plain pink and powder blue dress, her hair braided and tied up with a large pink bow. One would think her a guest until they noticed her dirty bare feet chained at the ankles.

Gar wondered briefly if she would jump this time. Each time she came to his chambers, she would stare out at the garden, her body tensing as if she were going to make a run for it. It was a 30-foot drop to the ground and he knew without question that her magyk, whatever spell she had in mind, wouldn't save her from breaking both legs.

"Tirin."

The girl continued to pace restlessly, her dainty hand at her mouth while she thought hard on her possibilities. Her eyes caught every flying bird that moved, every butterfly that fluttered from flower to flower. She wanted to be out of this place. Her levitating spell was her only hope for such an escape. Her inner debate was whether it was strong enough to keep her from hitting the ground too hard. Would it be strong enough to keep her off the ground?

"It won't."

Tirin rolled her eyes, finally remembering that the sorcerer was there.

"I think that your best bet is to wait."

Tirin sighed. Gar had saved her several times from being molested by Sayer and/or his guards, but something about him still kept her on edge. He seemed so wrong. Regardless of how cordial he was, she still found it hard to trust him.

"Don't want to wait." They were silent for a moment. "What do you want?" She finally faced him and watched him smile, an action that seemed strange for his face.

"Knowledge." He moved from his desk toward her. "Knowledge about Ao'lean."

She sighed again. "Do not believe I am wanted there," she replied softly.

"So you think they've abandoned you?"

He could practically see her heart break as he finished his sentence. Apparently it was something she thought, but could not say. She stared out over the balcony again.

Did her father truly never want to see her again? Had Tyrus given up on her when he saw her...kiss...?

"I..." Her hands quickly covered her face and her shoulders dropped. Gar moved closer, still waiting for an answer to his question.

"Tirin?" He nearly fell back as she turned to him with her face streaked with tears.

"I don't know what to think!" She threw herself at him, wrapping her arms around him and burying her face into his chest. Gar stood rigid, not sure how to respond. He searched the room for something to pry her off with, not liking the feeling that was welling up within him.

Sayer pulled away from the peephole, the threat of a very ungentlemanly-like guffaw ready to free itself and expose his hiding place.

He balked for a moment. Was Gar falling for the half-breed? *Could* Gar actually fall for her? All this time he thought the sorcerer too involved in magyk to be affected by lust or love or even just curiosity or conquest. Sayer quietly headed back up the narrow passageway toward his private chambers. The question was: was he jealous? Sayer felt irritated and betrayed that after his graceful treatment of the girl and all the gifts he'd given her, she had yet to say two pleasant words to him, let alone allow him to touch her.

He shut the hidden door and headed toward the door at the far end of his room.

It didn't matter. Gar and Tirin had to suffer for their actions.

Sayer was there at the door to greet them on their way out when Gar decided to return her to the dungeons. Prince Sayer smiled then bowed low.

"Any chance I can have your company for lunch, Tirin?"

Gar knew she was going to refuse without hesitation and nudged her sharply as she opened her mouth to decline.

She nodded instead, but not before Gar watched the Prince's eyes show his true feelings. He observed the two while they headed toward the dining wing. She was in trouble.

Lunch was a fiasco and as she recalled the events she knew that Sayer had done it all on purpose, to publicly humiliate her in front of all those people.

She just laid there on her straw mat, calling up the looks on the faces of those pompous humans. It all started when he asked about her necklace. She told him it was from her mother. Then he wanted to see it, and she of course said no. Whatever mood he was in was made worse at that. They watched him toy with her, put his hands where they didn't belong, and then have the nerve to kiss her. Of course she slapped him and he seemed so surprised. Prince Sayer reacted like a spoiled brat. In a rage he hit her, knocking her to the floor, threatening to do more, but then gasps from the 'ladies' stopped him. He called the guards in to take his gifts back, nearly stripping her bare before forcefully returning her to her cell.

She didn't care, much. She sat up and crawled over toward the center of her cell where water pooled. Looking at her reflection, she touched the darkening bruise on her cheek. It still stung, but tomorrow would find her with not a sign of abuse. She sat back and sighed, a new train of thought pushing her trouble with the prince back.

All this time she thought her fast healing was due to her human blood. Same for her sharper than normal sight, her high endurance and stamina. The heightened sense of smell should have been her clue, but as she'd never met another human being before now, she didn't know that her senses weren't normal for humans either.

Tirin crawled over to her bedding. Tyrus wasn't cursed. She knew this now, as a curse was personal, couldn't be altered, and couldn't be shared unless created to do so. But abilities could. They could be altered or diminished and she should have known that the very first day of his change. That moment she forced him to regain his form she had unconsciously given some of herself to him and she had taken a bit of him into her.

What would have happened if she hadn't done that? Would he have remained a wolf? She sighed again, realizing that all her wondering didn't matter. No one was coming for her. She closed her eyes, hoping that she would sleep forever.

Gar didn't know what to make of the ruckus coming from Tirin's cell as he made his way down the drab corridor the next day. Murai, Tirin's caretaker, was slumped against the wall far from the girl's cell when he finally reached the room.

Inside Tirin screeched as three guards tried to subdue her.

"What are you animals doing?" Gar bellowed, yanking one off by his throat. "Stop what you're doing now before I—" The guards pulled away from Tirin quickly.

Tirin glared at the three guards then looked at the sorcerer, panting heavily. Her face was dark with bruises and scratched but her throat was worse for wear. She couldn't seem to take Gar's shock anymore and broke into tears.

"What the hell were you idiots doing?" he growled.

"Prince Sayer wanted her necklace. We were ordered to take it," the bravest of the three said arrogantly, sporting bloody furrows on his face.

"Tell your prince that he is a fool. It's a spell catcher, and *no* one can remove the necklace except the wearer."

"Then tell her to remove it," the carrot top piped up from behind the first guard.

Gar put his hand on Tirin's shoulder and moved her closer to him. "That wouldn't help him. The necklace would become nothing more than a simple necklace. The spells caught would disappear." He dabbed at Tirin's face with his sleeve, wiping her bloodied nose. "Go tell your prince that he should have asked me before attempting this."

"Prince Sayer doesn't have to ask permission from—"

There was a flash and the third guard was gone. In his place was a sorry-looking goat. "Tell Sayer what I said," Gar finished.

The other two guards rushed out with the armored goat following, bleating pitifully.

Tirin pulled away from Gar, her whimpering tapering off. "I told him couldn't remove it yesterday. Why would he want my necklace?" Her hand went to her neck.

Gar frowned. "His attention is no longer on you. Didn't think he would find something new this fast."

Tirin was distracted by moaning outside the still open cell door.

"Murai!" With Tirin's attention no longer on Gar, the sorcerer couldn't seem to understand his sudden rise of jealousy. He followed her out and watched her tend to the old guard's head.

"They attacked you or you tried to stop them?" Gar asked in his normal cold tone. Tirin looked at him then returned her attention back to Murai, helping the old man to his feet. The old guard hugged her with a tender smile and Tirin accepted it without hesitation. Gar cocked his head at this.

"Hm." Gar straightened his robes. "Tirin."

The girl in mention turned to him.

"Prince Sayer is a brute. Things are only going to get worse from here on."

Murai shook his head and stood straighter. "You have to do omething'…Sir."

Gar found himself smiling at the sudden bravado from the old man.

"Really?"

Murai Dun was just an old guard, this job forced on him because he had been too drunk at the time to realize what he was agreeing to. He was the whipping boy of the castle. Most of the time he was drunk, so he never knew what was going on until too late. He wasn't happy when he sobered up enough to realize what he had signed on to do. But the rumors and the stories about Tirin were quickly quelled and dismissed after the first week he spent with her.

Tirin was a darling, suspicious of everyone, but her situation didn't make it easy for her.

Murai began to take to her. She reminded him of his daughter, the one who'd died, the reason for his drinking.

Murai nodded. "I o'erheard Prince Sayer tellin' some of his toadies that he couldn't believe how jealous he's grown o'er the relationship you 'nd Tirin have. He's not happy that she's closer to you than she is to him."

"Has he seen the way you two interact?" Gar almost laughed. "But I'm not surprised; he is still a boy mentally."

Murai sighed. "Sir, he is goin' to get violent, I fear for her. You have to do omething'."

The sorcerer rubbed his chin, amazed at the old man's gall. "What am I to do? If your brat prince is this jealous, it is only a matter of time before he finds a way to keep me from seeing her." He paced. The guard was right though; Sayer had surprised them all with how patient he had been with Tirin this far. This could only mean that she was going to be in serious trouble when he finally gave up and it could only end badly for her. Gar didn't want to see her hurt or molested in any way. He had yet to figure out how she acquired her magyk and where she was keeping the final piece to his own research.

"I'll try to come up with something." He turned to Tirin. "Until then, be nice and hide that spell catcher of yours."

Tirin watched Gar's back till he disappeared around a corner. "Where is my Tyrus?" she cried. "Why aren't they here for me?"

Murai hugged her.

*****

Tyrus loped back through M'kor Woods, his excitement almost getting the best of him. In two more days, a month would have passed since Tirin's kidnapping. It had taken their group a week in the wrong direction and then another two to correct that error. Sire Baelor had really laid into Darec for misleading them. It made Tyrus feel better to know that Sire Baelor didn't think the brat prince to be beyond perfect like most rank blind fools. After they returned to Ao'lean and made their way in the right direction, Tyrus quickly picked up the hunting party's fading scent. The trail took another four days to piece together after almost two weeks of being scattered and broken by weather and fauna. But Tyrus found it and on his own, after demanding that he take to searching the towns without the aid of Darec. Out of sight, he used his newfound control of his 'curse' to change into the wolf he'd always been, but with a twist. He could alter his color and size now, resembling more a ragged stray dog than the monstrous wolf. He picked up more gossip and rumors this way, not to mention better food than the rations back at camp.

The trail of broken information led them to the sprawling town of Norin, where the populace was mostly scholars and scientists of sorts. Their minds were more open than most and he was able to walk in without fear of being shot on sight, but after a few hours of being there he felt being shot would have been better. Getting a simple answer from these people was excruciating, for they preferred long drawn-out answers that wound about like angry snakes. But his patience won: finally a solid lead!

Abrupt warmth around his right foreleg brought his scattered attention back to the present. He quickly twisted in mid-leap, the bright blue glow of his adornment near blinding as he flipped sideways from an old rain-rusted bear trap. The sun was sinking and his heart thudded in his chest. The trap had been made obvious after years of neglect but like most, it would still break an animal's leg if set off. Tyrus sat down for a moment to calm his nerves. That had been close. He couldn't let his excitement get to him like that again. The blue glow gradually faded away and he quietly thanked Tirin for giving him the armlet. It had been the very first gift she had ever given him.

A year after he had been 'cursed' and his mother had died, he had moved in with the Desgjins. Soon afterwards, his early morning trips to Noir Swamps began. One day he blundered angrily into a trap and returned home a bleeding mess. Tirin fussed and tended to him for hours and when night came, she left at her usual time, but returned late the next morning. He listened from his room as she labored up the stairs, dropped something at his bedroom door, and then made her way into her room. She didn't come out of her room for almost two days afterwards. The bag at his door held this armlet and a note demanding he wear it immediately after a description of what it was to do. It warned him of harm and somehow deterred malice. He never understood how, he just knew he had to test it out. Of course, upon his return from his 'experimenting', somehow she knew, and more chiding was received.

Tyrus gave the trap one last look before starting again, but not before he surprised himself with a long mournful howl. How he missed her! He had never been separated from her for longer than a day. He missed hearing her laugh, seeing her smile, feeling her touch, the smell of her!

Tyrus ran at full tilt with renewed urgency. It had been too long without her. Time seem to speed up as he raced through the forest back to camp.

He smelled the smoke of a flourishing campfire as he drew nearer to camp. He was sure that despite his current demeanor, Baelor would be worried about him as he had left without telling anyone.

Evergreen watched when Tyrus ran through camp then noticed the contemplating look Alce was giving him when he passed them. The boy seemed more comfortable when a wolf now.

"Sire!" Tyrus barked. "She is in the next town!"

He panted heavily as he padded over to the older elf. "Kiten. Tirin is there in Kiten."

Baelor frowned. Kiten was a human settlement with little tolerance of other races. They saw non-humans as oddities or commodities. He started to ask him if he was sure when Darec sat up from his mat with a sour look on his face.

"How would you...?" he started, openly irritated.

Alce laughed aloud. "The idea that you would actually doubt someone with senses that exceed your own is ridiculous."

Baelor hid his smile, surprised that the Young Lord would be so obvious with his jealousy. He found himself unconsciously patting Tyrus on the head and received a strange look for it.

"He's faster than we are on foot or on horseback," Alce said, counting off the reasons on his fingers. "He's able to get in and out of places we would stand out in, especially with you tagging along. I can't believe I have to explain this to you!" He laughed again.

Darec glared at the young mage. "Well, if he was so proficient at finding things why didn't he do that to begin with?"

Baelor stood up, growing annoyed with the bantering. "Because you wouldn't let anyone. Due to your misdirection, we were headed in the wrong direction for far too long! You refused to hear any ideas from anyone! Even your own guards!" He stared at him. "You say you care for my daughter, but you'll have to excuse my skepticism of your sincerity, as you've done nothing but prolong this rescue and you were our only lead!" he snapped, growing angrier with each word. "You are practically useless!"

"Sire," Tyrus said quietly. Baelor took a deep breath and slowly released it.

"Let's go. I want my daughter."

Night had fallen almost five hours ago and there had been no word from Gar or Sayer since this morning's excitement. Murai had been called away almost seven hours ago, which left her with nothing to do but nap off and on in her isolated cell. Tirin had started to doze off again when Murai woke her with the frantic clattering of keys. She sat up abruptly, watching the door, immediately awake and ready for anything.

Murai finally got the door open, her dinner nearly falling to the floor as he seemed more rattled than normal.

"Okay, Murai?"

"Yes, girl, but you may not be."

"What is it?"

Murai calmed himself by taking a few deep breaths. "Gar is gone."

Tirin looked at him, confused. "What?"

"They escorted the sorcerer out an hour ago. After a right splendid argument with the prince." The old guard moved to kneel in front of her. "Gar tried to tell the prince that he needed you for some private experiments and the prince went mad! He started yellin' about some conspiracy between you and him and that it was not goin' to happen." Murai looked at the brown-skinned girl sorrowfully. "He said that you were his and he wasn't givin' you up, not till he was done with you."

Tirin's skin became clammy at the thought of her strongest ally being taken from her. But she felt that Gar was stupid in his assumption that the prince would so casually give her to him on loan! At the back of her mind, something told her that the sorcerer had done this on purpose.

"He's upstairs gettin' right drunk. He'll visit you sometime tonight. I don't know what to do, Tirin." The old guard paced the cell. "There is no other way out of here save the stairs, and after they escorted the sorcerer out under armed guard, he posted more guards at the entrance to the dungeons. There's no escape that I can think of."

Tirin found herself strangely calm as she watched Murai pace. Gradually her calm bled into anger at herself, all the years she'd been experimenting with different spells and yet her grasp of magyk was weak. Nothing she could think of would get her out of this fix. She would have to wait until the prince came to her.

"Fear this is last night here," she whispered and smiled slightly at the fearful look on Murai's face. "But I won't go alone."

Antoinette J. Houston

CHAPTER THIRTEEN

Escape

The elven party rode hard through the night. Kiten was only a few hours away. Midnight was quickly approaching and by the time they got there, the town should be well asleep, perfect for sneaking in and out without too much excitement.

Alce couldn't keep his thoughts and eyes off the elven prince as they followed his guards. What would the Young Lord of Ao'lean do once they got to Kiten? His mood had degraded to bare tolerance since they turned around. The young mage knew there was something …wrong? Maybe. Darec's whole demeanor was disturbing.

--- *Whaht is it, my lahve?* --- Evergreen's syrupy voice tickled through his mind as they zigzagged their horses through the trees. Alce briefly remembered the pain it used to cause him when she spoke to him this way. It was an ancient way of communicating, one that all elves used to use thousands of years ago, but no more. Now it was only the Ferine way of communicating.

--- *The Brat. His mind isn't right. I don't think it'll be long until he mimics his mother.* ---

--- *Meening?* ---

--- *His mother killed herself.* --- Alce didn't have to see the look of surprise on his mate's face to know it was there. --- *After killing ten others.* ---

Evergreen pushed her horse faster to match that of her lover's bay.

--- *His mother wahs ah Furii?* ---

Furii was a mental ailment that erased the ability to tell right from wrong. It caused the sufferer to enjoy pain for themselves but even more inflicting it onto others. Alce recalled the terror of the High Lady's last days, how one of the most graceful of ladies, the most beautiful of souls, quickly changed to easily rival the evil intent of a Core Devil. They had found the bodies of the missing servants when the eighth victim vanished. The ninth and tenth were killed on the spot when she was cornered and told what she was. Furiis never liked hearing about what they were or how they used to be.

--- *Yes.* ---

--- *You think thaht Dahrec will follow ahfter his mother?* ---

Alce mentally sighed. --- *I have no doubt.* ---

Baelor watched the mental exchange between Alce and his Ferine mate. His own was mind racing as fast as the horses they rode. What would she look like? How had her treatment been since he practically forced her into the hands of her kidnappers? Horrific images filled his head.

"Do not dwell, Sire," Tyrus hissed from Baelor's right side, his red mare, Talon, keeping pace easily. "It will not help." He knew what the old Imperial was thinking as his own mind was dwelling on the same things. He wondered what torture her captors had put her through once they realized she was a half-breed, a half-breed with magykal capabilities. With her stubborn streak, he was sure she would make someone mad. His heart sank a little as he wondered if she had given up on rescue with all the time that had passed. He hoped not. He recalled the torture Baelor told him he was put through by humans. Tirin was beautiful, delicate, and just as prideful as her father. Tyrus turned his attention to the race ahead. Suicide would not be a problem for her, he felt.

Kiten was closer now. 'Tirin, we are coming...*I* am coming,' he thought.

Darec stared blankly at Daynel's back as the group continued to speed forward. The Desgjins were proud and Tirin would more than likely keep to herself what he had done to her so many years ago. But she could possibly mention the fact that he had thrown her from his horse. It was going to be torture when she rejoined them...*if* she rejoined them. He could always stir up trouble upon their arrival.

Prince Sayer came just as Murai said he would, the ruckus outside her cell telling her that he didn't come alone.

"Open the door." The prince's words were slurred, full of alcohol, arrogance, and smoldering anger.

"Sire. She's just a girl," Murai pleaded with him pathetically. Tirin sat up, holding her breath.

"Open. The. Door," Sayer growled.

Tirin didn't have to be there to know that the prince's steel blue eyes were narrowed with rage.

"Suh-Sire, please."

"Are you defying me?" Sayer's voice was shrill.

She quickly stood up, pressing her back against the far wall of her cell as the sound of scuffling was heard at her cell door. She flinched at the sound of a sword being drawn and quickly covered her ears. Her eyes shut tightly till they ached. It took her a moment to realize she was crying.

All of a sudden, a ringed hand clapped over her mouth. Hit with a sudden flash of Darec planting that foul-smelling rag over her face, she screamed.

Her neck grew surprisingly warm and she knew that somehow, she had activated her mother's necklace.

Antoinette J. Houston

*****

"I still don't see why we have to leave the horses," Darec complained as he tied Necrom's reins to a tree.

"They would call too much attention to us, not being like the horses of this region," Zeph explained. "I think we look strange enough as it is to these…people." He carefully worded his ending. Baelor nodded at him.

"But it's dark, they won't be looking at a bunch of cloaked travelers," Darec continued.

"Enough," Alce cut in. "Morning is coming fast, let's get in and get out."

"Right, but we have no idea where she's been taken," Darec continued to complain. "Tyrus, go and sniff her out."

Tyrus growled loudly as he started for the Young Lord. Baelor put his hand on the boy's shoulder, surprised at the Tyrus' sudden eagerness to fight.

"Now is not the time for your childishness, Darec," the older elf hissed. "We have to work together and carefully. Fortunately, that means you have to stop acting like a spoiled brat!"

Evergreen silenced them with a shrill and eerie whistle. "Now is best time ta leeve, naht ahrgue…"

"Yes." Baelor sighed, almost ashamed. "Yes, we should be going."

They started to head off when the sound of scratching was finally heard. The scratching forced them to look behind them and realize that the redhead wasn't with them.

"Lady Daynel?" Rane called, a little concerned.

She poked her head from behind a tree; her small blade quickly returning to its hiding place in the folds of her dress.

"Coming."

Tirin's eyes readjusted as the light faded. She knew immediately she was no longer in her cell, as the sound of trickling water was gone. She was now in the armory.

She fell to her knees, misery overtaking her. She had no idea what to do with her new circumstances, but she knew that poor Murai…she knew he was dead. She fought off the tears that threatened and forced herself to stand up. She looked around and paused as she noticed her reflection in the highly polished surface of a suit of armor. Touching her necklace, she moved closer to inspect it, nodding as she saw that two of the once-bright stones were dull now, the Earth's pearl and the star rock. Something told her that Sayer had been punished.

Tirin bent down and picked up her clinking chain as she moved to the door. The sound of rushed footsteps brought her back to her predicament.

"--demon girl escaped!"

"--turned the Prince to stone!"

She quickly pulled back as a group of guards rushed past the door. She pushed her creeping fear back and urged herself to calm down.

"What now?" She looked around the large room, weapons of all types glinting at her coldly. She didn't know how to use any of them. She relaxed the grip she had on her chain before she rushed over to a rack of hatchets and took one, recalling a spell she'd memorized from the many notes that littered Gar's private quarters.

"Let's see if I can do this." She sat upon the cold stone floor, spreading her legs apart as far as the chain would allow. Holding the weapon with both hands, she raised it above her head.

Silently she invoked the spell, wincing as the chain began to quickly transform. She lowered the hatchet sharply.

The elves entered Kiten with no problem: the gate was unmanned. As they made their way further into town, they realized that something was happening. Torches could be seen darting here and there; guards were searching fervently for something…or someone.

"She's escaped," Baelor whispered more to himself, but he knew that Tyrus had heard him as the cloaked figure beside him turned to face him.

"What's happening?" Daynel asked, wrapping her cloak tighter around her as guards brushed past her rudely, ignoring her.

"Tirin's escaped," Alce informed them in a faraway voice. They all turned to him and saw that his eyes are closed. "We need to find our way to the castle." He opened his eyes quickly. "But be ready."

Tirin ran full tilt up the now empty corridor, her bare feet making no sound against the cold stone. The chain had practically exploded when the weapon smashed into it. Metal had changed to glass and she had underestimated her own strength. Shards of glass had entered her legs, face, and hands, some of it changing back into metal, but she forced herself to ignore it. The sound had been louder than she thought and she had jumped up to hide, burying larger shards into her bare feet. When no one came to investigate, she tended to herself as quickly as she could, removing as much as she could before feeling the need to run. The cloth ripped from her ragged maid's dress was already soaked with blood, small rivulets coursing down her legs. Someone would find and follow the small bloody footprints eventually; she had to find an exit soon. She pressed herself against the wall as she neared a corner. The smell of her own blood nearly blocked everything else as she tried to use the abilities given her through Tyrus. As she inched to the corner, she almost missed the smell of leather and metal from behind her. The two guards and Tirin stared at each other for a second before the taller of the guards yelled out.

"She's here! We've found her!"

She took off around the corner, hoping that there was no one in the adjoining hall, only to nearly run into a handful of them answering the alert. They stopped at the center of the other hallway as they saw her.

Tirin growled when she was cornered in the elbow of the two corridors. Without pause she turned and ran through the stained-glass window behind her, ready with a levitating spell, as she had no idea how high she was from the ground. The glass cleared and her bare feet hit night-cooled stone of a vast balcony. She scanned the area, the torch light enough for her to see clearly while she kept running. The guards were minutes behind her. She ran to the railing and quickly climbed over, watching the guards pause as she nimbly made her way across a narrow ledge to the next balcony.

The band of elves knew they were nearing the castle as the number of guards gradually increased. Darec found himself becoming more and more anxious. If he was going to do something, he had to do it now. He needed something to make them retreat or get chased out. They were traveling in a tight line, following the shadows so as not to become the new subjects of the searching guards. Darec sped up just enough to catch Daynel's cloak underfoot. She squeaked before falling into Rane.

A small group of guards turned their way, one of them trying to peer into the shadows that hid them.

"You! Over there! Come out!"

"Alce," Evergreen whispered. Her lover reached out and touched her still-sheathed blade. They all heard a strange hum.

The guards started to cross the street when someone yelled out of sight, "--they've found her and she's trying to make a run for it! Back to the castle!" The guards quickly forgot the shadow-hidden group.

"Follow them," Baelor whispered.

Thirty feet. Thirty feet. Tirin was beginning to hate that approximate measurement. Every drop she came to was too far for her to take safely. She wanted to be able to run to her freedom, not hobble away and get caught again. Not that she could do that either. Her legs were numb and the slivers had wreaked havoc she hadn't counted on. She was dizzy, tired, and lost. Tirin fought back the tears, again. She had found a moment of peace away from the chase after cutting through a large ballroom, which took her clear across the castle she her guessed.

The scent of hay suddenly hit her.

"Horses," she whispered, her breath hitching. The stables were in a separate building. She could jump from the balcony to the lower roof of the stables. She peeked from her hiding place. Should she dare to head toward there? She winced as she forced herself to stand; her legs weren't going to take too much more of this. Tirin took a shuddery breath. If she couldn't make it to the stables, she just wouldn't make it.

"Move," she growled to herself. She moved, stiffly at first, but then she heard yelling as she reached another window and moved faster. They had found her again. She moved quickly to the narrow ledge that seemed to connect every balcony this castle had, adrenaline racing through her. The throbbing pain of her feet and legs faded as she saw moving torches. She inched her way over the ledge and clambered over a small balcony when she heard a sound that froze her blood. She spun uncontrollably and hit the ground, hellfire ripping through her upper arm. She looked at her left arm, unable to fight the tears that filled her eyes now. An arrow had carved its way across her arm just above her elbow. Anger rose in her chest quickly and she regretted it, but allowed it to fill her. The thudding of feet filled the adjoining room to the balcony. Before they made it to the window, Tirin pulled herself up by the banister and met the faces of ten guards. Hate filled all of their eyes. One of them started to open the ornamental doors.

With a shrill scream, she flung her hands forward, and the doors, along with the guards, vanished in a large cloud of smoke and electricity. Stone and mortar exploded, throwing her over to the next balcony. As gracefully as she could, she rolled with the fall, returning to her feet quickly and running for the edge of the new balcony. Another scream tore free of her, this time filled with searing pain before she fell to the ground again. The pain was mind-numbing as the shaft of an arrow protruded from her right thigh. They were toying with her. She growled, feeling her strength fading fast, and knew she was losing it. She made herself get up. They needed her, probably thinking that she knew of a way to return their prince to flesh. She fell against the railing and turned to face the guards who dared to come near her. She had wanted to get out of here without the use of magyk, as her abilities had never been tested in situations like this. With her emotions volleying from fear to anger and back, she knew she couldn't control the amount of energy taken from her. She would pass out either way now, from blood loss or from the drain of energy. She hugged the mental image of her father one last time and apologized to Tyrus for the way things played out.

"*Hsseaf,*" she whispered. The spell conjured a stiff wind that lifted her before turning into a gale of destructive force that she directed toward her unwanted company. Most of them were blown off the balcony, its ornate structure no longer impressive as chunks of it were pulled away from the main body.

"*O~arreal!*" she screamed, holding her hands out in front of her. A disc of spinning fire quickly grew from hand-sized to about five feet across as it flew through the dispersing group of guards and into the castle itself, setting things aflame.

Tirin struggled to turn away from the now-flaming gaping hole in the side of the castle, her energy spent. Fire was always the worst energy drain of all spells. She dragged herself over the railing then went still; the smell of horses was close but...

Her eyes opened wide as not ten feet away from her, a strange and ominous shadow moved quickly up the side of the stable wall, scaring the horses with its presence. It moved toward her, its limbs disjointed and wrong. She swallowed, fear brushing away her earlier anger. Then the wind changed and her eyes widened.

CHAPTER FOURTEEN

Blood

"Blood," is all they heard him say before Tyrus rushed away from the group.

"Tyrus!" Darec yelled after him, drawing the attention of unwanted eyes. They all watched as Tyrus leapt from the street to the wall of the nearest house to get over the small barricade of shocked guards blocking the gates to the castle grounds.

Baelor swallowed as his eyes followed the boy, the cloaked and shadowed figure quickly moving across the courtyard to the stables at the front of the castle.

Alce smiled as he exposed his now-glowing hands. Guards surrounded them now and Evergreen was smiling, ready for some excitement as her blade pulsed with whatever power had Alce given it. Zeph and Rane readied their own weapons without a word. Daynel pressed her face into Baelor's back, but he couldn't tear his eyes from the small form running across the balconies. He watched her spin and fall, his heart catching, as he knew that something had hit her. He could hear her scream as she somehow caused the balcony to explode. His eyes caught the slight movement of the quick-moving shadow that was Tyrus. The boy moved up the wall as if he was nothing more than a wraith. Baelor said a prayer to all gods listening to his heart. 'Let the boy reach her, please.'

Tyrus ignored the frightened whinnying of the horses below him as he reached the roof of the stables. Her blood sang to him, and it sang of hate, and anger. He urged his body to change a little more, increasing his agility and strength, as he knew he was going to need it. He was fighting hard to restrain his anger as he saw how bloodied she was. He started; her body seemed to have gained a mind of its own as she suddenly rose from her slumped position. Then he realized she'd cast another spell. Tyrus kept still as the spell sent men flying over the railing to certain injury, if not death. The wind was still howling when she let loose a scream that cut at him. The next spell reminded him of her state of mind when she was thirteen. He watched the wheel of flames that spun crazily in the air before her before crashing into the dining hall.

He finally inched forward as she sluggishly turned around and dragged herself over the railing. She couldn't take anymore. Then he remembered that he was more than likely a strange sight to behold. His heart stopped for a second. Would she attack him? He sensed her sudden rise of fear as she finally noticed him. He listened to her rapid breathing and erratic heartbeat. The amount of blood that trailed back the way she'd come alarmed him. She was drunk with exhaustion. What had they done to her? Why was she in this condition? He observed her pregnant pause while she studied him cautiously and then she did something strange. She lifted her head to smell the air and shuddered.

"Tyrus?" Her eyes took on a wild look, a smile growing across her face. "Tyrus!" she shrieked hysterically. She started toward him only to stumble and nearly fall off the narrow ledge she was forcing her way across.

"Tirrin!" he yelled, frightened. He was too close to retrieving her for her to simply fall now. "Stay wherrre you arre!" She wouldn't make it to him.

The world was slowly spinning around her; her heart was beating so loud in her ears she couldn't think. Tirin pressed herself flat against the wall. Somehow she had made it over the balcony railing, but she didn't remember climbing it. She laughed suddenly. Tyrus was here, or was he just her imagination? She didn't care; this madness would soon be over.

The ledge crumbled a bit as she started to inch toward him. She gave a small shriek, pressing her back to the wall.

"Do not move!" he growled.

She stiffened. "It really is you."

He focused on her face. The smell of her tears was sharp at first before mingling in with the scent of her blood.

"I-I thought you had...thought you were angry with me...so angry." She sobbed pitifully. "Thought you never wanted..."

"Shh." He made sure of his footing before moving. "Never." He rushed across the ledge. Mere inches from her, he felt a sudden joy as he stretched his hand out and she reached for him.

"Ty--!"

His growing smile died as a meaty 'thunk' silenced her. Her eyes widened in shock before her hand fell back to her side. His insides felt as if they were being wrenched free of his body as he saw the arrow now lodged in her chest.

*****

A sharp mournful howl caused Baelor to pull his eyes away from their fighting. The old Imperial watched as Tyrus' cloaked form rushed past them and the attacking guards. Frighteningly fast, the boy leapt from the wall to the roofs and disappeared into the night. Baelor's heart knew something was wrong. He swallowed.

"Time to go." He nudged Daynel behind him, trying to keep her in the center of the group as she whimpered.

Zeph and Rane kept the guards at bay with ease. Arcs of light flew from Alce's fingertips while he laughed maniacally. "She let loose some serious spells."

Darec found himself frozen in his spot as he watched Tyrus vanish into the night.

Evergreen nudged him, calling his attention back to their situation before sending three guards flying with a guttural yell. The elves paused when they finally heard Daynel hysterically chanting. The redhead bent, touching the flat of her palm to the ground.

Alce smiled knowingly. "I knew you were making--"

The gathering guards pulled back as the ground beneath the elves' feet was suddenly etched in fiery markings before the intruders disappeared in a flash of red flames.

Gar almost laughed aloud as the spell ignited a few of the surrounding buildings. The caster was a novice; the recall spell could have easily destroyed this whole section of the city.

He silently turned and headed back to his own horse. Gar was heading back to the castle to retrieve Tirin by force; a wicked smile played on his lips. He was surprised and a little disappointed to see the small elven rescue party here. They hadn't forgotten about her as she'd thought.

He had arrived too late, not thinking that Sayer would make his move so soon on the girl. The excitement had been going on for over an hour by the time he returned; all he could do was watch and assist a little bit. Deflecting the arrows was easy, somewhat, weighing them down so that their numbers dwindled drastically to the stray one or two that may have hit her instead of the original twenty. The last arrow almost hit its intended mark. He was distracted when the strange elf came into play. That peculiar elf startled him with his wraith-like movements.

Gar looked back at the smoldering section of the city where Tirin's rescuers had been. He raised a brow in curiosity at the gathered abilities. This generation of elves seemed to have become more unique in talent. There were two magyk users, one a wyld mage and the other a pyromancer. And then there was the wraith that wasn't a wraith. Gar could swear that he had been normal when he was with the group but his body…changed. Interesting.

But the one that interested him the most was a face he hadn't thought he would see again, at least not alive. This face was the reason for Gar's charade for the last 80 years. Baelor Desgjin. What was Tirin's connection with the imperial guard? He rubbed his chin; he would find out eventually. Tirin had something he wanted.

*****

"--a glyph!" Alce finished as the flames died.

The tree Daynel had been scratching on before they made their way into Kiten now stood in the center of the group. An area ten feet in diameter around the tree was now nothing but ash.

Alce smiled as he touched what used to be a tree. "But you need more practice. I can…hm." His blood-red eyes turned an amused yellow as he saw that the prissy elf passed out in Rane's arms.

"Tyrus!" Baelor began shouting. "Tyrus!"

Alce's smile faded as a long desolate howl answered his call. He immediately knew the girl had to be hurt. They followed quickly as Baelor ran toward the howl, heading back toward Kiten.

With his heart in his throat, Baelor called again. "Tyrus?"

"Herr-re!"

All of them rushed toward the strange gravelly voice and all but Baelor, Alce, and Evergreen paused when they reached him.

Tyrus stood away from Tirin's motionless form.

He was not in wolf guise. Darec and Daynel looked at each other and then back at Tyrus' new form. They didn't know whether to be shocked or very afraid at what stood before them. Tyrus' cloak hid all but the evil rapier-like claws that held his cloak tight about him. He had gotten at least two feet taller; his new form was hunched and threatening. His legs were angled wrong as he moved nervously further back. His enlarged violet eyes glinted apprehensively from the darkness of his cowl as he sensed their uneasiness at his appearance.

"Rrremoved arr-rrows," Tyrus growled.

Alce bent down next to Tirin, a slight smile appearing as the girl he remembered from childhood somehow retained that defiant pout even on her more grown-up face. He touched the wounds and couldn't help but be impressed with Tyrus' skill even with the wicked claws he was sporting now. The hairs on Alce's neck rose as a sound he never thought he would live to hear gradually became louder.

The older elf was crying. Alce found he couldn't look at Sire Baelor as he took in the damage to his daughter's body. "Oh, Cattea..."

Tirin was in bad shape. Her earth-brown skin was ashen and dozens of cuts and gashes covered her legs and arms. The worst of them were still weeping bright red blood. Her feet were horrific, with colored glass deeply embedded in the tender flesh, darkly coated in a mixture of dirt and blood.

Alce moved to kneel next to Baelor, his crying tapering off as he caressed his daughter's face.

Alce took Baelor's hand and placed it on Tirin. "Picture her the way she was before all this."

Baelor closed his eyes.

Alce laid next to Tirin, interlacing his fingers with hers. He got comfortable on the ground, feeling the curious eyes of everyone else.

"Don't touch me until I'm done." He closed his eyes.

"Ahlce." Evergreen moved closer.

"I'll be okay." He opened his cerulean orbs, reassuring her with a smile before closing his eyes again.

Baelor watched as the Alce slowed his breathing, inhaling through his nose and slowly exhaling through his mouth. For a moment Baelor thought the boy had gone to sleep until Alce's eyes snapped open, revealing nothing but a soft white glow.

The sensation was immediate and the old imperial almost pulled away when it encompassed him. It surged through his daughter and up his arm.

"Can't we move--?" Darec started, stopping when he saw Alce's glowing eyes. He looked up to see Tyrus melt into the shadows of the waning night.

Did he always have such control over his transformations? He continued to gaze at where Tyrus had been standing, recalling how Tyrus had partially transformed back in Kiten. How was he still standing on two legs when most of his life saw him on four? Darec pulled at his lower lip thoughtfully. Tyrus' change had come on quickly as well, frighteningly fast. He had never watched him change, though he was always curious about what happened when he did. Did it hurt? He walked toward Zeph, ignoring Rane, as the younger guard seemed too preoccupied with the limp form of Daynel now.

"Horses," the Young Lord said frankly. "Apparently this will be camp."

CHAPTER FIFTEEN

The Truth

Baelor watched in slight amazement as the shallow cuts and lighter bruises on his daughter gradually faded. Those, he knew, were easy. His eyes grudgingly drifted over to the hideous gash on her arm, watching as slowly the bleeding tapered off, then stopped completely.

Evergreen silently sat near Alce and calmly removed her sword to clean it. The whole camp was silent as the night wore on. The events slowly faded to be replaced with questions of what would happen next.

Baelor looked up from his precious daughter, seeing the Ferine's eyes glued to the blond elf. Her hands were steadily cleaning her massive blade without hesitation even though her mind was elsewhere.

"Yes?"

Baelor almost flinched at her sudden attention. "Am I necessary?" he asked, keeping his hand on Tirin's chest.

"Yes." Her deep green eyes pulled away from him and back to Alce. "He...he will need yor energy."

Baelor looked at his daughter's still ashen face.

"Chance of death?"

Evergreen's white brows rose high on her forehead, causing her iridescent skin to shimmer slightly. "Fo' her? No. Fo' Ahlce, yes…fo' you …due to yor ahge…yes."

Baelor gave her a small smile; if he had to die, he would without hesitation. He nodded his understanding. The sensation that connected him with the fragile girl of his blood and Alce ebbed and flowed like the ocean. Sometimes it swelled strongly like a threatening roar, causing a sense of dizziness, only to then soften and pull away from him like an ending kiss. The night waned calmly, quietly, and slowly. Despite the group's silence, morning stole over them as the old Imperial's body finally gave in to his exhaustion, his hand stubbornly still in contact with his sleeping daughter.

Tyrus finally returned from wherever he had vanished in full lupine form. He padded silently to lie at Tirin's feet, ignoring the protective glare of Evergreen.

Darec awakened hours later as the forest's fauna stirred. The sky was painted with deep purples and pinks as the smell of cooking meat chased the lingering sleep from the young prince's body. He slowly rolled onto his side and took notice of the older guard.

Zeph stirred the steaming pot silently, smiling slyly as he watched the younger guard flirt coyly with a blushing Daynel.

Darec almost felt jealous.

The sun rose and traveled across the sky, but no one seemed to be in a rush now that Tirin was no longer in serious danger. No one even seemed to be concerned that they were still mere miles away from an angry town whose prince had been turned into a lecherously grinning statue.

So Darec simply waited and watched.

Sire Baelor was still out cold alongside his half-breed daughter and the annoying mage. Evergreen was still watching everyone else with a distrustful gaze. Not worried like a fretful lover, but keenly, like a cat ready to pounce.

Tyrus was irritating him. The Young Lord's thoughts were jarred by the idea that Tyrus had utter control over his transformations. When did that happen? How? Had it always been that way?

Darec chewed on his thumb thoughtfully. It had to have been Alce. The dog-boy had never had such confidence until after returning with the weird wizard. That pain in the ass had to have done something to ease the worry and concern usually burdening Tyrus. He was dangerous now, Darec admitted without pause. He was showing emotion with ease and without concern, and Darec couldn't have that.

Tyrus raised his head then turned to face the stirring Imperial.

The older elf sighed, looking about, mildly disoriented, before looking down at his daughter. He sighed again, caressing her face. Her color was much better than last night. Immediately he vowed never to push her away, never to let her go off angry, or alone for that matter.

Hearing a sniff at his feet, Baelor looked to the wolf, surprise crossing his face when he finally noticed Tyrus.

"I am sorry, Sire."

Baelor raised an eyebrow. He was surprised to see the boy in full wolf form. He recalled the monstrous form from last night and concluded that Alce had definitely done something to the boy or to his confidence.

"Sorry?"

The wolf fidgeted nervously. "I...did not get to her...soon enough." His eyes seemed glued to Tirin's dirty bare feet.

"Tyrus." Baelor gave a slight groan as he moved to face him, feeling every bit of his 182 years. "You didn't shoot her."

"But--"

The old imperial ruffled Tyrus' mane, causing the wolf to quiet.

"You got her back for me."

They became silent for a while before Baelor reached over and caressed Tirin's face again. He regarded Alce, concerned, noting the boy's eyes were no longer open. He looked up to Evergreen. "Is he--?"

"Sleeping." Evergreen nodded. She didn't think it prudent to mention that Alce had stopped breathing at one point during the night. "Ahlthough." She knelt down and touched Alce's arm. "He won't be of much use for ah day or two."

"I'm sorry for the trouble." He watched her eyes widen at his words. Apparently she wasn't used to such gentle treatment. "Not all of us surface dwellers are disrespectful," he assured her. She gave him a slight smile and nod.

"Mm."

Tyrus' head snapped up at the soft groan.

Baelor leaned closer to his daughter, his heart skipping. He wasn't all that sure that the noise had come from her.

"Tirin?"

The girl just barely opened her eyes, the swirling colors and fuzzy forms slowly coming into focus.

No one moved, no one made a sound. Her eyes slowly opened wide as she recognized the form hovering over her.

"Fa--?" Her voice cracked and tears streamed down her face as Baelor pulled her to his chest, hugging her tightly.

"Shh." He rocked her, tenderly rubbing her hair as her body shook uncontrollably with sobs. *"Cattea, na blauta pue moa,"* he whispered, nuzzling her cheek. *"Alah fe...alah fe lo moa."*

Daynel watched quietly, a lump in her throat as the scene played out before her. Her own father had never showed her such...adoration, saying such expressions were a show of weakness. But Tirin was anything but weak. Stubborn through all the bullying, she showed nothing but strength and determination. Daynel turned away from the emotional show. The tears wanted to come and she was fighting hard against them. She knew she would never be able to look at Tirin the way she used to.

Darec found it interesting that he felt absolutely nothing. At least until Tyrus crawled up by her side and started licking her hand, slowly getting her to pet his head.

"Dumb dog," Darec hissed to himself, only to watch startled as the 'dog' in mention glared at him with teeth bared.

Baelor rocked with his daughter, listening to her sob, feeling her tremble against him. He never wanted to feel this again. Never.

The day passed with little excitement. Alce slept through it all, but as the day ended he stirred. He had enough energy to be half walked/half carried and pushed up onto Evergreen's horse as they headed toward home. By nightfall the camp had been dismantled and the fire dead for almost two hours when Gar finally reached it. He smiled in the direction they were headed. This would be easy.

The trek back was slow, deliberately. Baelor rode in silence, still cradling Tirin. Tyrus walked solemnly alongside, staying close to them, whispering soft words to her. Alce was snoring slightly against Evergreen's back, more than likely drooling, from the strange look on her face. The guards were up ahead, talking quietly to each other, Daynel intermittently joining in.

Darec merely watched. Tirin would eventually get over her shock and talk of everything. What could he possibly do to prevent this from happening?

He watched as Tirin's fingers brushed across Tyrus' face, causing the dog-boy to hesitate for a brief second. He then dipped his head forward, bashfully hiding his face in a black curtain of his wild hair.

"Can we camp? I'm tired." Darec forced out through clenched teeth, wrenching his eyes from the strange family.

Tirin's eyes met his. She loosened her grip on her father before Tyrus reached up to help her down, her dark eyes locking with his.

Tonight.

Evergreen placed Alce's hands on his chest after laying him out on the sleeping mat. She paused for a second before realizing that she was being watched. She turned to watch as the old Imperial's daughter slowly walked over to where she and Alce were bedding down. It struck her as odd. Evergreen knew that all the girl had to do was ask and her father or Tyrus would have carried her to them. Instead, with a determined glare to her very human eyes, she made her way on her own. The flesh of her feet was obviously still tender, with the care she took with each step. Even though they appeared healed, her soles would take another day or two to be completely mended.

Tirin finally reached the couple. Her tongue stuck out of her mouth at a quirky angle while a small smile played across her face. "Finally. It didn't look to be that far!" she huffed.

Evergreen looked at her, then almost smiled as she saw the look on the girl's face as she stared at her. It was weird and it almost made Evergreen laugh in amazement. Tirin didn't look at her like the others did. Her eyes held no notice of her obvious difference from the rest of them. It was like she saw her as an equal.

"Thank you."

Evergreen blinked. "Oo?"

Tirin smiled. "Thank you. For coming with them. To...to save me."

The Ferine slowly cocked her head to the side. "Yor welcome."

Tirin grinned at her. "Lady Evergre--"

That was taking it a little too far for her. Evergreen snorted, amused. "You ahre tha Lady here, Lady Tirin. Such titles ahre waysted on me."

"I don't think so." Tirin resituated herself, looking and feeling more normal. She was glad her father had packed some of her clothing. After she awoke in her father's arm, and calmed down a bit, she had him burn the maid's uniform she had been wearing. She was more than ready to forget that part of her life.

Evergreen observed Tirin quietly. The mixed girl tenderly took Alce's hand and watched his sleeping face. Unsurprisingly hestirred.

"Mmphf." Colorless eyes opened to spy her. He smiled, a soft cheerful yellow delicately coloring his eyes. "Tirin."

"Alce." She leaned over and hugged him tightly, then quickly pulled away to pinch his nose. His light yellow eyes darkened to gold.

"Wha--?"

"Where have you been?" Tirin's gentle air was quickly replaced with playful ire. Evergreen sat at his shoulder with a smile on her face as the two friends renewed an old relationship.

"All this time you've been safe."

Alce yawned, his eyes switching to fuchsia before he sat up. "Tirin. I'm glad to see you, too." He grinned.

"You should be."

Baelor watched the exchange with a smile, glad that his daughter was refusing to dwell on the past. It would take time for her to discuss what had happened, but he didn't mind. She would never again berate herself for the blood of her mother anymore. Not after meeting both the good and bad of her human side.

Tyrus looked on as she slowly tried to get back to normal. She would tell all as soon as she got over her skittishness. The sharp, acrid scent of fear was slowly being replaced with her normal smell of honey and caphony flowers. He closed his eyes, recalling her loving caress of his face earlier. It had startled him, almost caused him to stumble. He wanted more of that attention and knew he would get it. The look in her eyes now, when she turned to him. It was there. He could feel it. She loved him. Him. He opened his eyes and immediately found Darec studying him.

The Young Lord was not pleased. However, Tyrus couldn't tell if it was with him or Tirin, or both. He wanted to laugh, because he really didn't care. He redirected his attention to Tirin upon hearing her laugh at something Alce was saying. He delighted in seeing her smile, hearing the laughter he had missed so much. Drinking in the sentiment hidden behind the pull of her lips when she smiled when their gazes met, Tyrus sighed inwardly. He was whole again. The long-awaited confrontation with Darec would probably be sometime tonight. The prince couldn't seem to keep his glares hidden or his comments to himself. It only made Tyrus more anxious to put his fist to Darec's face.

Zeph watched as one by one the small party fell asleep. He looked up at the moon, sighing as he recalled looking up at the moon from his post at the gate. He had wanted some excitement…he definitely got it. He laughed softly before heading off to make the first circuit of the night; this adventure should keep him happy for maybe ten years before he needed a change of scenery again.

Tyrus sat up as Zeph's footsteps headed away from camp. Quickly he walked over to where Tirin laid. Smiling, he bent toward her, delicately brushing her outstretched fingers with his. Her hand curled close and she shifted to face him. Her sleep-blurred eyes spied him and a groggy smile spread across her face.

"Tyrus," she whispered before falling back to sleep.

He grinned wolfishly while watching her breathing slow. Tyrus felt the eyes of another and slowly turned to face a glaring Darec. Surprising even himself, Tyrus bared his fangs at him before darting off into the darkness. Darec clambered to his feet quickly to follow him.

Grumbling, Tirin sat up, rubbing her throbbing hand and glaring after Darec's retreating form. She massaged her ailing appendage and then noticed that Tyrus was gone as well. She quickly got up.

"You bastard!" Darec screamed into the night's air as somehow, somewhere, he had lost track of Tyrus. His insult echoed through the night without a rebuttal; he heard nothing but the sound of the wind through the trees.

A soft growl whirled him about and fingers of fear crawled across his stomach when he faced the darkness of the thick brush behind him. The night was given a pair of bright violet eyes when Tyrus made his whereabouts known.

"*I* am a bastard?" Tyrus rumbled.

"Yes," Darec snapped. "How long have you been planning on stabbing me in the back?"

Tyrus growled again. "I think it is the other way around...*Young Lord.*"

Darec looked at him, somewhat shocked by his bluntness. He wondered again what had brought all this about, especially since Tyrus seemed to be welcoming the release of pent-up emotions.

"Oh high and mighty master," Tyrus said caustically. "Dare I explain what I mean?" He cocked his head to the side as he came forward a few steps. He was enjoying this. He smiled as best he could with his transforming mouth.

Darec backed off when Tyrus gave him a menacing grin. He remained in the shadows, but Darec could see that Tyrus had yet to finish changing.

"The selfish, spoiled brat. The cause of my anguish." Tyrus drew closer, a frightening sight. He had more than doubled in mass and hair. The strange sounds Darec was hearing he recognized now as the popping and reshaping of Tyrus' bones. He gawked, seeing

Tyrus' flesh move as if it was about to separate and form another being. Darec wanted him to go back into the shadows, where he belonged.

"It is not the so-called curse I blame you for, but the so-called friendship you felt compelled to give me." Tyrus sensed Darec's discomfort at his appearance and moved closer to give him a better look. "I had thought we were friends once, but you made it clear that I was nothing but a flunky."

"Maybe," Darec hissed. "If it wasn't for me you would be…"

"You truly believe you had something to do with keeping me here or alive?" Tyrus finished. "No. I would have died because of my mother, because of the fright I caused those guards that night. The only one who saved me was Tirin."

"Whom *I* love…" Darec started, only to cut himself short when Tyrus lunged at him, resembling more the wolf now.

"Do not lie to me as you have lied to yourself!" Tyrus seethed. "You love the status she has earned, you love that she is special, but you do not love her!"

Darec glared at him. "What would you know?" he snapped, the little fear that had gripped him dispersing as his anger flared. "You say I've changed, but so have you."

Tyrus shook his massive head when his change reached its end. "Yes, into a wolf. Very observant." A strange grin seemed to settle on his canine face.

Darec's eyes narrowed in irritation. "You changed as much as I did."

"I changed because I had no choice. It was hard to remain who you once were when not only did you kill your own mother but to have those you once called friends and family turn their backs on you." Tyrus paced in front of him, his eyes never leaving Darec's face. The Young Lord only stared back at him.

"I tried to be your friend, this excuse…"

"Not an excuse, Darec. You were never my friend, actually. I was just another lackey you convinced to help you torture Tirin. Being a fool, I actually tried to get back into your good graces. I hated the isolation you and the rest of 'our friends' bestowed upon me after you told them I betrayed you after catching you..." Tyrus closed his eyes, unable to finish that line of thought. "And then when I failed at your dare and...changed. My relationship with Tirin strengthened, to your dismay. Even then, you knew that any chance of our being 'friends' was strained, but you did not want to chance my possible revelation of what you did to her father." He paused as Darec glared at him. "What you did to Tirin...I lost all respect for you then, but being young and stupid, I went along with it. And wanting no trouble as Tirin did not remember, I kept it to myself."

Darec turned away. "I didn't ask you to."

"No, you did not," he barked. "But you knew that I could not divulge such knowledge to anyone without being looked at as a brute." He bowed his head. "Blameworthy due to association." He pawed the ground, digging up a little of the grass. "That is the truth behind your attempt to secure Tirin for yourself: to keep all secrets silenced." Tyrus sat down upon his haunches, his tail whipping about. "You plan on using her as you have used me."

"What?"

"For a long time, I actually thought you were trying hard to fix what you had done, until you let it slip that you were appreciative of my silence weeks later after publicly proclaiming your friendship to the 'dog-boy'," Tyrus snapped. "You were using me to keep your reputation pristine by letting your guilt be my friend when no one else wanted to, just in case Alce let it be known what you had done. Lucky for you he was nowhere to be found."

Darec rolled his eyes. "I suppose you're going to blame that on me as well."

"I do not know. Should I?"

Darec kicked at him, watching as Tyrus scampered out of reach. "Maybe some of what you say is true. Maybe at one time I felt that if I had turned my back on you like everyone else had, you would have said something."

Tyrus sat with his back to him. "All those years of being your flunky and you had the audacity to think this?"

"Tyrus." Darec sighed. "It wasn't as easy as it seemed being the son of the High Lord. I had no true friends, no one I could trust. You were all just there to make yourselves look better."

The monstrous wolf shrugged. "Maybe in the beginning it started out that way. Befriend the young master, receive gifts and privileges that most cannot get. But after years and years and the faces of those you called friends changed, save mine, you could not see that I had matured to the point of truly being your friend?"

"No." Darec shook his head.

Tyrus sat there in silence.

Darec observed him, at first a little ashamed of the truth, then that faded. For a long time, he had felt like Tyrus was holding him back. In the beginning, it had been a good idea to keep him as an ally but as time wore on, it became a chore. Tyrus grew cold and near unfeeling, closing himself off from everyone. It became difficult to discern his emotions, and it was hard even pretending to be friends with a wall.

"Now that it is official that our association has ended," he said with some contempt, "are you going to stand in my way at every turn?"

Tyrus looked at him finally. "Most definitely."

Darec balled his fists. "Why? What does it matter to you? Even if you do love her, she can't possibly love you. No one can."

"The true colors of the Young Lord finally show," Tyrus growled. "All this time, you knew how I felt about her, yet continued to pursue her."

"Of course I knew. We may not be the best of friends, but I knew you once. Your feelings were becoming harder to read as time passed, but it was obvious to me how you felt toward Tirin. At first I thought it was just gratitude because of how she helped you but then..." Darec frowned, then shrugged off the explanation. "I've pitied you from the start, knowing your life was ruined forever. Who would want a dog for a husband?" He shook his head and gave a small sarcastic laugh. "Actually, you had a chance, though, at the Comne." Darec eyed him. "Tirin's desperate, or haven't you noticed that? She'll take anyone who's an elf to make sure she can keep calling that city her home. All you had to do was ask."

"The fact remains that I refuse to let you use her as you have used me," Tyrus said calmly even though he wanted so much to make him choke on what he had just said. He watched as Darec threw a fit. Shaking his fists and stomping his feet, Darec, the Lord of Ao'lean, threw a tantrum like a spoiled child.

Darec walked up to him and knelt so his face was level with Tyrus'.

"How am I going to use someone I love?" he yelled. "There is no way in hell you can prove that I don't love her."

"Besides the guilt you feel for raping her and the fear that the child could have been yours?" Tyrus asked evenly. Darec stood up.

"How do you know this?" Darec asked, confused, thinking that no one else knew save those concerned.

"I was there when you raped her, remember?" Tyrus watched as the Darec fidgeted. "Do you think because my body changes that my brain becomes like that of a dog as well?"

"The child was not mine, she said so."

The dog laughed arrogantly. "I know." His violet eyes stared holes through him. "I was there when she became pregnant. Besides the odd gestation period, believe me, it did not resemble you in the least." Tyrus paced a small circle around Darec, slowly making it wider. "You have only been concerned with the potential consequences of your actions. None of what you have done to befriend her meant a thing to you. You never cared for her. Now that you find out that she is half-elf with strong magykal abilities, you think she will make an acceptable trophy wife? I cannot believe you think her that simple."

"Ass."

Tyrus ignored his barb. "She had no idea what had happened to her after that, but you did not know because of your cowardly ways. You just want her to keep silent about how it could have been yours. Try and make her happy so she will not tell Sire Baelor. Shower her with gifts and compliments. Try to win her over so that one day you can ask her to forgive you."

"Shut up."

"You think she would ever forgive you?" Tyrus stared at him. "You think that after what you did, she can easily forget how you abused her? Actually turn her mistrust and contempt into love and adoration for you, you think you are that charming?"

Darec felt the urge to shut him up permanently as Tyrus laughed heartily. "Shut up."

"The shock of her first 'No' must have been traumatic because you cannot honestly believe that Tirin would ever forgive you, especially since you cannot forgive yourself." Tyrus backed away from Darec as he seemed ready to explode.

"Shut up!"

"You see? It is out of selfishness, not love, that you want her. You have no true feeling for her, so why would I let you try to sway her your way?" Tyrus watched Darec calm down, letting his words fade.

"I care about her, a lot." Darec swallowed as he glared at the dog. "I may not love her but I am more than confident that in time it will grow to be." He grinned at him arrogantly. "I am as charming as you care not to believe. Not only will she have me, but she will take me without question of my sincerity and her life will be better for it."

"You still plan on marrying her?" Tyrus asked, surprised.
"Yes."

Tyrus shook his head. "She has already told you 'No'."

Darec shook his head back at him. "You can't stop me."

"Why would you…?" Tyrus whispered.

"Does it matter?" Darec cut him off. "It's not like you would ever let your feelings out to show her how you feel, you overgrown icicle." Darec smiled at him. "You have been in love with her for the longest time, and you have done what with this affection? Buried it, just as you have buried every other emotion the great Gods have given you. Your fear, your paranoia of your curse keeps you from doing anything you want. You can be nothing to her, nothing but a very good guard dog."

Tyrus stood frozen, not sure if he should smile or frown. True, he could control his talent now, and he knew Tirin had feelings for him, but it was also true that she had yet to come to terms with it. But with Darec mentioning his fear, the dreams or nightmares…did they really mean anything, or were they the pranks of his paranoia?

"I can be more than you," he whispered.

Darec laughed. "A pet."

Tyrus glared at him. "A pet that will make sure you never get her hand," he snarled. "I will become a constant in her life, making sure there is no way in hell you can sway her heart your way. I will remind her of the horror you put her through. Keep fresh the insult you did."

They glared at each other. Tyrus threw his head back and released a howl, a long eerie howl of anguish that sent chills down Darec's spine as it echoed through the trees, silencing the night-time fauna.

"Why must you be so selfish?" Tyrus snapped. "Why not let someone who loves her…" He stopped as a smile slowly crawled across Darec's face.

"If anyone would hurt her, it would be you." He looked up into the night sky as he crossed his arms. "You refuse to let anyone in. I honestly believe that the Tyrus I knew long ago would have let me know about his feelings for her, despite the ridicule of others. You were stronger then, Tyrus, you always let everyone know how you felt about things and I honestly believe that I wouldn't have stood in your way to try and court her."

Tyrus snorted. "Mostly because you and others would have started torturing me as we tortured her."

Darec grinned, his right hand twirling a bit of hair. "This is true. I don't doubt that at all, but you would have taken it." His grin widened. "Now it's too late."

"It does not have to be," Tyrus said simply.

Darec stared at him suspiciously. "And I'm supposed to trust someone who has had nothing but contempt for me for the past," He begins counting on his fingers, "seven years? You've been holding in all this disgust for me for so long, Tyrus. What's to make me sure that you will not one day reveal that deep dark secret once you have secured the prize?"

"You cannot."

Darec eyes became narrow slits and his chestnut complexion became ruddy quickly.

"To hell with you, dog," Darec growled. "She's special. Life has some grand adventure for her and I want to be a part of it." He admitted. "Besides, the Grand Ao'lean revealed her in a…"

"That vision was nothing but your own fantasy. So selfish that you do not even remember that you made that up yourself," Tyrus snapped. "You care about nothing but gain for yourself." Tyrus narrowed his eyes at him. "You are just evil!"

Darec gawked then laughed uproariously. "Maybe next time you'll move a little faster!"

Tyrus whirled about, heading straight for him, his teeth bared fiercely and a hate-filled growl filling the air. Tyrus leapt into the air, ready to attack, and Darec's anger melted quickly into intense fear. He yelled out.

Darec fell back onto his rump, his own feet the cause of his unbalance. His arms over his face, Darec listened to his own yell taper off to a whine. He looked through the gap between his arms to see Tyrus standing less than a yard away from him, his hackles up, teeth still bared and a low yet vicious growl droning on, but the crazed look that had been in his eyes now gone.

"You stupid beast! How dare you..." Darec started only to scramble back as Tyrus darted forward, cutting him off.

"Shut up and leave me be!"

They stared at each other for a long, drawn-out minute before Darec got up and started back for camp. He grumbled loudly as he distanced himself from Tyrus.

CHAPTER SIXTEEN

Daynel

Tyrus was a fool. How dare he think that bringing up the past would actually make him feel unworthy of Tirin's hand? Darec remained silent as he continued to walk. The quiet of the night made his thoughts loud. The stillness of the brush surrounding him was unnerving as he moved through it. Careful not to snag anything, he maneuvered his way back toward camp, the sounds of the crickets and other nocturnal animals slowly muted by his pondering. Marrying her would be the ultimate sacrifice, the proof of his repentance even if she didn't want it. Darec looked ahead, unconsciously searching for shadows that didn't belong. In time, he knew his feelings would grow deep for Tirin, he was sure of it. She was special; the Grand Ao'lean had made it known that she was more than what her lineage showed. He wanted some of that attention.

Something moved ahead, causing him to stop.

"Who's there?" he snapped, watching the tight band of trees ahead of him. Darec saw the red of her hair even in the darkness as she came out of the shadows. "Daynel? What're you doing out here?"

Her glare was intense, making him uncomfortable quickly. "Sire Baelor awoke to find Tirin gone. He got worried that something may have happened, until he found that you and Tyrus had disappeared as well. Actually for a lot longer than she had." She moved closer toward him before continuing. "We decided to look for the three of you."

Darec blinked, confused. "Tirin's gone?"

Daynel's glare intensified. "You shouldn't worry. She's around here somewhere." She watched, almost pleased, as his façade showed a little apprehension.

Darec swallowed. "You heard everything, didn't you?" He knew the answer was yes as suddenly she broke into tears.

"As loud as his howls and your shouting were, it was hard not to!" She took a hitching breath and then threw her hands over her head, her eyes glaring up into the star-filled sky. "All I wanted was for you to see me, to see how much I was in love with you!" she exclaimed angrily.

Darec's mouth dropped. "Daynel…"

"I tried everything to convince your heart." She wiped her eyes. "I've been trying for the longest time to get you to look at me the way you pretend to look at her. I hated Tirin for you, tortured her to impress you." She sniffed loudly. "Then I hated her because she had you and she didn't seem to really want it, and now I know why." She sighed. "I remained faithful to my emotions, waiting for you to see me. I was sure that you would eventually grow out of your attraction to Tirin's humanity." She laughed. "I suffocated my life for you only to find out you're not what I thought you were." She shook her head in disappointment. "Now I just feel sorry for her."

Darec started to ask but her glare of utmost disgust silenced him.

"Because of you," she snapped.

"What?"

Her voice wavered as she moved even closer. "You raped her and actually think that marriage will make it all better?" She glared at him with such hatred he lost his reply.

He took a breath to start again.

"Shut. Up!" she snapped. "If that isn't bad enough, you don't even love her, and you actually believe that she's that desperate to belong?" She looked at him in disbelief, then grabbed him and shook him. "How could you?" She searched his face. "I had such respect for you! How in the world could you do that and believe that she'll marry you?"

Darec glowered at her, now irritated, before he pushed her away. "This is why I never found you attractive," he said exasperatedly. "You don't know when to mind your own business. Besides, I didn't ask you to do anything for me. Anything you've gone through was your own fault."

Daynel paused then laughed. "Listen to you! You think so high of yourself, trying to pretend you're so well-mannered when you're nothing but a low-class brute! You actually think that Tirin will take you for a husband? You took advantage of her, you monster!" She found it hard to keep her voice even as a painful lump found its way into her throat. "You hideous fiend!" Daynel screamed.

"None of this is your business." He looked at her coldly. "And you would do best to keep it to yourself."

"Are you threatening me?" She laughed again. Darec continued to threaten her with his narrowed eyes.

"She's a good person, whether I care to say so or not. For you to even think that this will make all her dreams come true is insulting to any civilized woman." She took a deep breath, then slowly let it out, trying to calm herself down. "You are truly not who I thought you were."

Darec remained quiet for a moment. "No one asked for your opinion, Daynel." He turned and started to walk away.

"Tyrus was right, you know!" she yelled after him. "You're a fool! A selfish dim-witted fool! This stupid plan of yours will never work!"

He stopped.

"You are an idiot to believe that she'll take you!"

Darec glared at her for a moment before storming over to her and grabbing her by her arm roughly.

"Will you be quiet?" he hissed, not wanting anyone else to hear this. "No matter what you think, Tirin will be happy with me despite whatever you or Tyrus think you will do." He shoved her away, feeling his temper beginning to boil over. "Besides, you're just upset because it's not you. Jealousy doesn't make you right."

She huffed, yet found it impossible to say what she wanted. She slapped him and then watched him smile rather bemusedly at her before slapping her back.

She held her face as if it was going to fall off, surprised that he'd done that. "I did care for you, but who…what woman in her *right mind* would want a *rapist* for a husband!" She backed off as his eyes took on a strange look. Keeping her tears in control, she continued. "I can apologize for the hell I've put her through and in time she can forgive me, but you can't." She grinned as the distance between them became substantial. "Every time she sees your face, hears your voice, she'll remember how you violated her."

"She'll forgive me," he said more to himself.

"She can't even if she wanted to, you idiot!" Daynel screamed. "You're a monster! Everything about you is insulting!"

Sudden hate for the redhead swelled up in his chest, so quick he could barely breathe. "You're pushing it."

"So? Tyrus deserves her. He's taken care of her even before he realized he cared for her. He's her true love and she'll see that soon, now that I've changed my ways!" She smiled at him. "I'm going to do my best to become her best friend! Like Tyrus, I'll make sure she never thinks about you romantically!" She faltered as the look on his face said more than she wanted to read. "Or anyone else for that matter."

"I'll kill you!" Darec raged as he ran at her, quickly cutting the distance between them. She screamed as he grabbed at her. Ducking and collecting her cumbersome dress, she took off ahead of him.

He watched as the air around her shimmered when she began working a spell. He threw himself at her, tackling her, interrupting the spell.

"This isn't going to make it any better!" She struggled to get her legs free enough to kick him away. She was able to get a quick kick in, drawing blood that only angered him more. He yelled as he grabbed her again, this time missing the only sign given when she worked a spell. She was too afraid to truly control it so it became more or less a distraction spell, but it worked. Flames swirled about him, blinding him momentarily and singeing him a bit. With a yell, he released her and she scrambled away. He grinned, knowing it would be quite some time before she could recharge for another spell. He sat there for a minute or two until his eyes refocused.

Daynel screamed as she ran. Baelor and the others were here somewhere, where she didn't know. She now regretted her urgency to find Darec first on her own. Daynel continued to run; how was she supposed to know that he was crazy? She tripped over a root and went flying, her scream choked as she got a mouth full of dirt. She cringed as pain shot through her head, spitting out both dirt and blood from biting the inside of her mouth. She scrambled up, looking behind her as her heart jumped into her throat. The air was still; the forest now seemed loud with agitated noise. The animals of the night seemed to have awakened to bear witness to her attack. Her fear intensified as the noise seemed to increase with each frantic beat of her heart. She zigzagged through the brush, cursing herself. Why such a small spell? She knew more detrimental magyk. She had to get her nerves under control. Pausing, she grasped her head, a headache threatening as she realized she was utterly lost.

"Sire!" she yelled frantically, knowing that Darec would find her faster but at the same time hoping that Sire Baelor or Alce would hear her and reach her first. "Sire Des—"

The way he held her head, her neck felt as if it would tear from her shoulders.

"Always running your mouth!" Darec growled from behind her. Daynel whimpered as he gripped her face harder. "This is why I don't like you!"

Daynel shrieked as he hit her twice then threw her down onto the ground. He straddled her, locking his hands around her throat.

She clawed his arms, trying to loosen his grip to no avail as the pressure increased.

CHAPTER SEVENTEEN

Nae Doashe

Tyrus stood there, stiff with anger, his glare glued to Darec's back as he walked off. His heart's rapid beat drowned out the Young Lord's fading grumbling. How he wanted to show Darec how bestial he could be. Tyrus remained still, a hard knot in his chest, the product of his denied anger, painfully expanding.

"How long are you going to hide there?" he asked, annoyed.

At first there was no activity and then the brush ahead of him began to move. She emerged slowly, her eyes on the ground as she moved toward him.

"I'm impressed with your restraint," Tirin said softly.

He made an irritated noise and turned away. "It was only because you were there."

Silence hung in the air like a thick fog. She knew how perturbed he was; he had always hated being spied on. "Are you mad?

Tyrus looked at her abruptly, startling her. "What do you think?" he snapped. "Because of you, I could not…" He sighed as he watched her bow her head. He curled his tail about him. "Tirin, I am sorry. I did not mean to…"

"It's okay," she mumbled. "If it makes you feel any better, part of me hoped that you would hurt him, regardless of his position." She looked at him. "As much as he has hurt you…"

"And you?" He gave her a sidelong glance.

She turned away from him, her body tensing with a combination of emotions. Slowly she turned back to face him.

"Yes." She raised her chin defiantly. "Are you ashamed that your heart longs for someone so vindictive?"

The fact that she knew of his feelings for her now proved enough to calm his anger. In fact, it filled him with slight humiliation, but there was no turning back now.

"After all he has done to you, I would expect no less," he answered quietly.

They stood there silently for a moment before she ran to him, embracing him and holding his head inches from her own, nose to nose.

She swallowed hard. "All because I thought it was all too good to be true and that this wouldn't last." She watched as Tyrus licked his nose. "I'm sorry for not realizing my feelings for you sooner, Tyrus. But I...I can never...accept Darec's proposal...the water at the Comne...it forced me to remember what he did..."

She let herself fall against him, burying her fingers in to his fur. She felt him take a slow breath before lowering his head to rest upon hers. "I do feel a sort of desperation...but it's for you..."

Tyrus sat there, shocked that she was being affectionate with him and while he was in lupine form. How foolish he suddenly felt for thinking that she would be disgusted and ashamed to do such a thing even though wolf and elf were the same.

She put her hands on either side of his head. "Revert."

Tyrus gave her a strange look as he heard her words in his head and in his ears. Comforting warmth spread through him before he felt his body going through its phases. He looked at her, surprised, as she stood up and went back to the bushes to retrieve what appeared to be his clothing. She knew his 'curse' was not a 'curse'!

With her back turned, Tirin tossed his clothing to him, then began to explain what had brought her out there.

"I was only being nosy," she admitted. "I had no idea what I was going to witness when I followed the two of you out here. I knew that Darec had always wanted to see you change, but I didn't know you were going to be out here berating each other." She sighed deeply and hesitated before saying more. "Darec stepped on me in his rush to pursue you, so I assumed that to be his reason in following you."

Tyrus stifled a laugh as he finished dressing.

"You may turn around," he said, shaking out his hair. "How long have you known?" he said, moving toward her. She gulped.

"Yu-you're not angry, are you?" She backed off but not before he caught her wrist. "It wasn't for too long. I wasn't trying to keep it from you!" She whimpered as he pulled her toward him. She watched his black claws curl about her arm. Their pointed tips caressed tingling trails along her skin.

"Tirin, you have nothing to worry about, I just want to know," he reassured her. "How did you figure it out?" His other hand wrapped about her other arm. Her breath stuck in her throat.

"I–It's just my opinion, but I don't think your curse is a true one. I think it's more or less your own true talent, your gift from the Grand Ao'lean. It's an ability passed through your family. More than likely skipping a generation or two and evolving with time." She swallowed as his eyes stared into hers. "Ah...I also think that by interfering, I may have...muddled it."

He cocked his head in mild confusion. "Muddled?" He watched as she searched his face. "It's more than likely my fault that you can't control your transformations." She averted her eyes, feeling guilty. "I know you know about my trips at night...to Wonderlost. I found a book of spells long ago and have been practicing from it since before I helped you. It's the safest place for my experimenting, but whatever I did to you, I included myself. I seem to have taken some of your gift and incorporated them into myself as well. Aspects of your gift become mine and when you change, they increase in sensitivity again."

Tyrus pulled her closer to him and heard her whisper breathlessly, "Oh, Tyrus." It brought a slow smile to his face. He found himself suddenly remembering a term from an ancient poem, one that had three meanings of love. *Nae Doashe*: My heart, my life, my everything. He didn't understand why, but the phrase wanted to spring from his lips in reference to her.

"I am in love with you," she whispered. He smiled broadly and watched as she daintily fanned herself with her hand. He grew alarmed when she swooned and he lowered her carefully to the ground. He cradled her to his chest as she fought to regain composure.

"What are you doing to me?" she whispered as he caressed her face. "Why am I feeling this way all of a sudden?"

Tyrus laughed and then shook his head. "I am doing nothing to warrant this reaction. I think it is because you are over-excited."

She took a deep breath, trying to steady her nerves, agreeing silently. "I…I realized my feelings before you left the Comne. I don't know why it…"

Tyrus kissed her forehead, silencing her. He observed her wide eyes, smiling at her reaction. She wasn't trying to get away from him and his courage strengthened as he held her against him. He felt her breath hitch when he kissed the side of her face and traced a line across her cheek with his finger. Her eyes shut slowly when he raised her chin, watching until the last moment when he kissed her full on the lips.

For a sustained moment they remained that way. He could hear his heart loudly in his chest; he could feel hers beating the same rhythm against him. His paranoia faded; his fears and doubts left him as she accepted him as he was, saying so with her beautiful mouth pressed against his as she wrapped her arms about him.

The kiss came to an end and he watched her duck her head bashfully, trying to hide the bright smile on her face.

They sat there silently, holding each other in the bright light of a full moon with the sounds of the forest night comforting them.

"When did you find out that you weren't cursed?" Tirin asked finally as she looked up into his content face.

Tyrus' grin widened as she did. "After I reunited with Alce. He explained everything to me when I finally made myself go to see Bayne…" He trailed off, his smile faltering as he remembered that Darec had kissed her. She sat up, as she knew that look.

"What?"

"Darec kissed you when…that is why I left…" he started and paused as her slight worry turned into a smile.

"Oh, so you did see that." She patted his face before she leaned back against him. She smiled as he admitted to spying on her, that he had left her because of jealousy. "In your rush to abandon me, you missed me slap him for his lewd behavior." She wrapped his arms back around her.

"You slapped him?"

Tirin nodded, then paused in thought. "Twice."

Tyrus looked at her in surprise. He was also a bit impressed. His brows furrowed in concern. "Did--?"

"He didn't hit me, he…" She held her face as she remembered the Comne. "Tyrus, I wish that night had never ended. I…" They sat in silence once again as both knew that nothing could be done about that.

"So what did Alce have to say about your…issue?" Tirin inquired.

Tyrus squeezed her and smiled. "That it is not a curse, but an ability that is passed to every other generation from my father's side."

She made a pleased noise. "Really? So I was right!"

"This is my gift," he agreed. "Originally, I was to permanently become a lupine monster, able to augment my wolf form, but unable to become myself again."

Tirin looked at him in surprise. "What?"

Tyrus hugged her. "I am not entirely sure how Alce knows all this from just one visit, but he said that we have a connection, a bond of some sort. This connection let us know each other. I do not know exactly how it works or its extent. To be truthful, I became angry with you, thinking that this was your way of repaying me for all the hell I put you through. That you were making me feel the way I do about you, making me a slave in a way, but Alce informed me otherwise." He caressed her face as she sat in his arms in awe. "He said it is you that made it possible for me to revert back. He did not explain that you and I would make an unconscious trade, some of your humanity for some of my lupine aspects; I do not think he knows this. But you are the reason I can still call myself an elf." He pondered a little before he hugged her again. "He told me that I can control it if I wanted to."

"Extraordinary," she whispered.

"What?" He raised a brow as she stared at him.

"In all the time I've known you, you have never talked so much!" She grinned when he rolled his eyes at her. She then became pensive.

"As far as this connection...will I...?"

Tyrus shrugged. "Besides the heightened senses you experience now, I do not think you will begin changing form or growing hair."

Tirin gently stood up and waited for him to stand with her. When he did, she put her hands behind her back and looked thoughtfully at him. "So, you can control your change?"

He nodded. "And apparently so can you." He smiled. "And I know now the reason for my having aspects of my alter form, the teeth, the nails, the senses. Alce said that I had to free the wolf every now and then. Because I refused it for so long, it began to...bleed through, to find other ways to release itself."

The suspicious smirk growing on her lips hinted at mischief.

"Tirin," he said warningly.

"Now that you can control it," she said, moving toward him. "You won't think or believe that you'll hurt me anymore?"

Tyrus' face dropped. "What?" The vividness of his nightmares came rushing back to him. Is their connection so strong that she could see his dreams?

"The nightmare you have almost every other night." She paused. "You've screamed my name several times, followed with 'what have I done?'"

Tyrus looked away from her, ashamed. He always believed that he was able to wake himself before they got too bad. Neither did he know that he spoke so clearly in his sleep. "I thought...I did not know..."

Tirin hugged him, saying nothing.

"I no longer believe that I can harm you." He mumbled into her hair before kissing the top of her head.

"You should know that sometimes..." She paused, gauging his sudden stillness. "I've entered your room when you are in the throes of a nightmare. That's how I know."

He sighed, for some strange reason relieved. He hugged her tightly. "We really should be returning to camp." He grinned as she groaned.

"Do we have to?" she whined.

He nodded. "Right after I kiss you. Nae Doashe."

Tirin felt warm all over as he said the last. He had just leaned in to kiss her when there was a shrill shriek. They looked at each other, knowing it had to be Daynel. Without a word, both rushed toward the scream.

CHAPTER EIGHTEEN

Furii

Baelor crashed through the brush as he heard the shriek, Alce and the others close behind him as he followed the echo. His heart couldn't take it if Tirin was in trouble again. He prayed silently as they ran, vowing to never let her go anywhere without protection. If he was not with her, she would go nowhere. If Tyrus was not with her, she could go nowhere. Even if Darec wasn't with...

Baelor couldn't believe what he was seeing; it was as if the boy was possessed. His eyes had a crazed look while he seemed only concerned with killing Daynel. Darec's sleeves had been ripped away by Daynel's clawing, revealing deep furrows that bled freely. Baelor finally moved as Daynel's arms fell limply to either side.

"Darec!" Baelor yelled as he ran at him. The Young Lord turned, his wild countenance changing as he was startled and sent flying when the older elf kicked him.

"It's not what you think!" Darec screamed hysterically, clutching his side. "She attacked me!" Baelor ignored him, turning instead to give aid to Daynel.

Darec watched while the redhead was revived quickly, revealing that she had feigned death, to his dismay. He yelled as he started back toward Baelor and Daynel, determined to finish what he started.

Baelor had just pulled his blade free when the guards, Zeph and Rane, appeared. Not sure what was going on yet knowing the Young Lord's temper, they restrained him. He struggled wildly to get loose, to no avail.

"She's possessed or something!" he screamed, his self-control failing even more.

Alce and Evergreen finally showed up to see Daynel slowly sitting up as if from a fitful sleep, Sire Baelor armed and ready, and the two guards holding Darec.

"What is going on here?" Alce asked, approaching Baelor. The older elf soundlessly pointed at Daynel who slowly turned to face him. He froze when he saw her bruised face and the angry red blotches on her neck. Then he looked at Darec, whose shirt sleeves were in ribbons and the skin beneath scarlet with blood.

"It looked ahs if you wahre right, lahve," Evergreen remarked, seeing the same.

Alce shook his head, a confusion of emotions within. He was excited that his theory had been correct but appalled at how it had proven itself.

"He was right about what?" Zeph asked guardedly.

Alce walked over to the hysterical Darec and observed him closely. "This rotten brat's like his mother." He watched as Darec stilled his angst. "He's a Furii."

Darec looked frantically from Alce to Baelor. He shook his head.

Baelor's eyes widened in shock. "Are you sure?"

Alce nodded. "It's yet to take over fully, but he's…"

"No, you fool! Th–that's not it at all!" Darec struggled with the two guards as they suddenly increased their hold of him. "Daynel…she was trying to…"

Alce glared at him. "Don't deny your heritage, boy," he snapped. "Your words aren't believable even if I were wrong." He walked away, a small smile on his face. "And I'm not."

Darec released a small strangled 'no' before falling to his knees. Was he like his mother? Had he inherited what killed her? He grabbed his head, threatening to pull his hair out. Was he a Furii?

Tirin and Tyrus approached carefully, shocked at what they observed. Darec seemed to be losing his mind, falling to the ground, his hands wrapped about his head as if it pained him. Tyrus urged her to be silent as she started to make the others aware of their presence. She turned to ask why when he pointed to her father. She saw him helping Daynel to her feet. Tirin gasped as she saw the bruises on Daynel's face and the condition of her clothing. Had Darec done that? She looked at the hysterical Darec and noticed the still-bleeding furrows through the tatters of his sleeves and forced Tyrus to follow her.

"What's happening?" Tirin asked as she and Tyrus approached.

Darec looked up to see Tirin and Tyrus walking toward Baelor, with Tyrus holding her hand.

He exploded.

Alce watched, alarmed, as the Young Lord attacked both Rane and Zeph, quickly taking them down with violent accuracy. "She's mine! I told you, she's--!"

Tyrus started to meet Darec head on when something forced him back. Alce's hands danced for a moment before Darec went flying. He slammed into a tree and seemed stuck to it.

Alce grinned as he admired his handiwork, although his magykal energy was still low so he could already feel the strain. "Not a chance, boy. Tirin has more sense than that."

Darec kicked and raved like a lunatic. "No!" He screamed. "She is mine! I've already had her!"

Alce's face dropped, as did his concentration, and for a second Darec was free. He fell to the ground with a painful thud, not realizing what had happened until Alce got his wits back about him and pinned him where he lay.

Tirin looked from Darec to her father, who looked at Darec, confused. "What?"

Darec's eyes widened as he realized what he had said. He remained quiet.

Alce brushed loose strands of hair back, feeling suddenly nauseous. "S-Sire…"

Baelor started toward Darec, then stopped halfway, turning to look at Tirin.

"Tirin?"

"He…he's the o-…one you're…" Daynel croaked then swallowed hard. "He raped her."

"Daynel!" Alce hissed, alarmed at her readiness to reveal all.

Baelor's eyes went wide with disbelief as he looked at his daughter. Tirin couldn't meet his gaze, finding the ground a more welcoming sight.

Evergreen started for Alce as her love suddenly and startlingly fell out of character, acting like a small child caught kicking the family dog.

"It was my fault, Sire," Alce said. "It was when I was weaker. Darec took a vial of sleeping…"

Baelor looked at him so coldly Alce quieted. "So in your fear, you ran away instead of coming to inform me."

Alce looked to Tirin for aid but she was still enthralled with the ground.

"Believe me, Sire, had I known that he would do such…I didn't know he was going to hurt her!" he pleaded. "I…I was in the woods…waiting for her…we…I couldn't do anything then…"

"Is this true, *Cattea*?" He took a step toward her and watched her back off, hiding behind Tyrus. "You said you weren't…" He looked at Tyrus and watched the boy raise his chin boldly.

"You knew, didn't you?" Baelor strode over to them, hearing Tirin whimper as he did. Tyrus took one step back as the older elf stood in front of him. "Of course you knew!" he growled. "You stayed in my house, ate my food, took advantage of my charity, and you kept this from me?" Baelor raged.

Tirin watched as her father's fist tightened. "No, Father, don't!"

Tyrus pushed her back before Baelor hit him. He rocked back a little, his hand going to his mouth as the pain fogged his sight. He tried to shake it off as he saw Baelor getting ready for another, then Tirin stood between them. She pushed Baelor back.

"You will not hit him again!" she cried. "If you need to hit anyone it should be me. I'm the one who lied to you!"

He slapped her, silencing her. Baelor looked at his daughter, then Tyrus, who still held his mouth. "I can't...how could you keep this from me?" he hissed at her. "Not only that, but you actually befriended him, had me believing that you three had become the best of friends! Moreover, you lied to me! You said you weren't raped!" He turned away from her and glared at Tyrus. "And you! His sidekick for the longest time, allied with that, that *Mubeswae*! You abused my hospitality, my taking you in--"

"Sire Desgjin, I did not mean for any of--"

"Tyrus has no loyalty to Darec; he hasn't for a long time." Tirin looked at her father with tears in her eyes, still holding her face. "But you have taken his respect for you and thrown it in his face, just now."

"Tirin!" Tyrus and Baelor said in unison.

"You shouldn't take advantage of Tyrus' loyalty to you! That's not fair!" she yelled. "The pregnancy was not his doing. Because of my anger, I tried a spell I had no right to try! It took my memory of the whole ordeal, up until the Comne. Father, the water made me remember, it's not that I was trying to keep it from you. I had no idea 'til then."

Baelor glared at her for a moment, then grabbed her and hugged her tightly. "What makes you so special that you can take these who have treated you so badly and befriend them?" He kissed his daughter's ear as he continued. "I love you so much, *Cattea*, have watched you struggle with the likes of them throughout the years." He shook his head, not wanting to look at either Darec or Tyrus. "Not interfering because you never asked, but for you to keep this from me, it will be some time before I can get over this." He swallowed, urging her to follow as he whispered. "So, what you were telling me in the Garden?"

"Yes," she whispers.

Tears threatened as he nodded. She hugged him tightly, shaking her head.

"Father, that was my own doing. It was a spell gone wrong. I can explain that." He sighed, somewhat relieved yet still a little disturbed. Baelor patted her on the head, then turned, his eyes finding Darec quickly. "And you!" he said in a deadly tone, his anger rising again quickly. Alce watched, rightfully afraid as Baelor moved through the guards as if they weren't there to go after Darec. His sword free, Baelor was going to punish or kill the Young Lord, as would have been his right if Darec were anybody else's son.

Evergreen was his only obstacle.

Baelor glared evilly at the girl watching as she stood her ground, her own weapon by her side.

"Move, child," he said simply, raising his weapon threateningly.

She shook her head and braced herself. "You need to cahlm yo'self. Killin'im will do nahthing bot make it wose fo you."

"That needn't concern you," he started. He watched, annoyed, as she shook her head again.

"Whaht wood hahppen win yo high lod found thaht his frieend killed his only son? Will he be sympahthetic o will he be vengeful ahs well?"

Baelor stared at her for a long moment then raised his sword, yelling all the curses he knew before stabbing the weapon into the ground beside him. Evergreen's broadsword remained by her side. They all watched as Baelor moved forward toward Darec, his hand a tight fist.

"You can't touch me!" Darec struggled to get free, keeping an eye on Baelor's hand as it started to rise. "You can't touch me!" he screamed.

Baelor stood there in front of him, his face contorted in anger. "You are a waste of flesh!" Baelor snarled. "Your father's name is shamed with you as a son." He lowered his arm. "You should not exist and if it was up to me you wouldn't!"

Darec's fear was quickly replaced with smugness, the laws guarding his status filling him with arrogance. "So what's stopping you, old man?" He grinned.

"This will kill your father, but he will find out." Baelor looked at the boy, pity and fury battling it out inside him. "Being his only son, I can't do anything about it."

"In other words, get the hell away from me!" Darec looked at the two guards. "Get over here and release me!"

Alce walked slowly toward the young prince, his eyes a deep crimson. They held an evil shine as he moved in front of the two guards.

"Only those who are loyal to your father and that miserable city can't touch you," Alce piped up, an odd smile now forming on his face, making his cold expression a fearful one.

Darec looked at him, his smugness fading. "You...you can't..."

"I have no loyalty to either," Alce finished as he moved closer.

"Rane! Zeph! Restrain him!" Darec's voice cracked. To his horror, he watched as both guards turned their backs.

Alce smiled, his eyes flashing a range of colors. "I don't think anyone will mind if I take what's rightfully mine."

CHAPTER NINETEEN

Run!

Daynel smiled secretly at the battered Darec as they walked back to camp. She had no idea she'd feel as pleased as she had when Alce began beating Darec. But she did. She saw it in Tirin's face as well.

Daynel dropped her head. If only she had been there. Regardless of how she felt about Tirin's humanity, she would have stopped him from doing that. She knew, in her heart, that she would have gone as far as using her skills on their Young Lord to prevent him from doing something so vile. She took a deep breath, her throat still a little sore from Darec's attempt to kill her. She knew it would be a while before her feelings for him totally faded, but she did not care. She would free herself of him.

They paraded back through the woods toward camp in silence. Darec, bound and gagged, was being led by a tether held by Zeph. Daynel caught his glare again and found slight enjoyment in sticking her tongue out at him. Darec's growl was muffled as he walked between his guards.

Alce was the happiest they'd ever seen as he practically skipped back with Evergreen in tow. Tyrus and Tirin brought up the rear, with Baelor keeping step behind them. Tyrus looked up from Tirin to find Daynel looking at him. He let his eyes speak for him and thankfully she understood. Daynel walked back toward them and took Tirin's hand. Tirin looked at the redhead, surprised.

"Tirin, can I talk to you?"

Tirin smiled warily, then nodded. Daynel grinned and led her away, giving a quick glance to Tyrus.

Tyrus bowed his head as his pace slowed.

"I'm not apologizing for hitting you, Tyrus," Baelor said suddenly. "You deserved that and more." He watched as Tyrus sighed.

The younger elf looked him square in the eyes. "I am not looking for an apology, Sire. I am the one who should be apologizing. I did take advantage of your hospitality when not being honest with you, but you should understand that I plan on taking something else as compensation for my pain and humiliation."

Baelor looked at him in disbelief. "You are overstepping your boundaries, son!" he snapped.

"No, Sire. I am not. True, I kept a secret from you after all you have done for me, but only because of Tirin. For me to betray the trust of your daughter would have been far worse than your anger with me now."

Baelor looked toward his daughter, amused to see that she was watching him as well. "You may be correct in that assumption. You are more than just a friend to her. To lose your loyalty would've crushed her." He looked back at Tyrus. "But do not assume that all is forgiven. You knew this secret far before you befriended my daughter and you could've told me then. I assume your alliance to Darec prevented you fro--"

"Yes, it did. But reluctantly," Tyrus answered. "Sire, I wish for you to forgive me and to understand that I meant no disrespect. I hold you in high reverence, far higher than that of our High Lord." He looked away. "No one has done more for me than you or Tirin, and this is something I will never forget."

Baelor raised a brow in growing surprise as he saw a blush rise on Tyrus' face. Were his eyes playing tricks on him, or was the light of the moon causing an illusion? Or was this really a blush?

"I take it the floodgate of your emotions has finally taken all it can." He almost smiled. "What is it that you want for retribution?"

"Your confidentiality." He looked at him pleadingly. "I would like your daughter's hand…" He trailed off as Baelor stopped in his tracks. "Sire Desgjin, please do not make me beg."

Baelor looked at him in disbelief. "Make you beg?" He wanted to laugh, but knew the boy was already too humiliated now to handle it. "Make you beg?" he asked again incredulously. "Tyrus, you and Tirin were meant for each other. Neither of you realized it, but rest assured I did."

He put his hand on the boy's shoulder. "I know the hell you went through with your curse. I know about the nightmares you suffered, boy." He smiled slightly when Tyrus bowed his head just enough to shield his face with his unbound hair. "However, I also know the love you showed my daughter despite your need to wall in your emotions." Baelor waited until Tyrus peered at him through his curtain of hair. "Watching you two was the most aggravating thing a father could go through. Both of you were agonizing over things that you had no control over, yet finding relief in each other without even knowing it. Make you beg." This time he did laugh. "You have tortured yourselves enough."

He gently turned Tyrus back toward camp, ready to resume their walking. "But I am curious." Baelor glanced over at Tyrus, whose mouth simply hung open. "Why is this secret?"

Tyrus swallowed, then took a breath. "Tirin does not know…I am not ready for her to know my desire just yet." He took another breath as he looked at the old Imperial. "I have nothing…to give …"

Baelor shook his head, frowning. "Not true."

"Sire. I cannot live in the house where my mother died." He paused and pulled a clawed hand through his curls nervously. "I have no occupation, no income."

"All you have to do is ask." The older elf sighed before starting again. "But something tells me that Tirin won't be staying in Ao'lean."

Tyrus raised an eyebrow.

Tirin feigned listening with amazement to Daynel. Starting with a heartfelt apology, the redhead continued on and on and on about what she had gone through throughout the years. Tirin wanted to be a courteous listener but was unable to keep up with her incessant babbling. Daynel's words ended up going in one ear and out the other.

Tirin continued to allow the other girl to lead her by her arm behind the two guards and Darec. Carefully picking the right pauses to nod at, she kept her attention on the two men trailing behind the group. She couldn't help but worry as Tyrus' unbound hair hid his face and her father wore the biggest grin she had ever seen. She gave a quick glance to Alce and groaned slightly as the his smile mirrored that of her father's. His pleased pink eyes quickly turned a vicious red as he stopped suddenly. Tirin paused to ask what was wrong when she sensed it as well.

Baelor and Zeph stop dead in their tracks before looking at each other.

There was not a sound. The waking fauna was now dead silent.

"Someone invoked a major spell," Alce hissed, his red eyes scanning the surrounding trees.

Tirin shivered suddenly, shaking her head as she gripped Daynel's arm tightly, causing the girl to whimper.

"No."

Rane looked at her with concern. "Lady Tirin?"

Baelor watched as his daughter shuddered again, shaking her head while she looked about frantically. "What is it, Cattea?"

"How could I forget? How could I forget?" She looked at her father. "Goblins, Father. Goblins live here!"

Their reaction was immediate. Baelor and Zeph drew their swords as Rane grabbed Daynel and Tyrus grabbed Tirin. All of them began running.

"Gib me ah sord!" Darec yelled around his gag and Alce laughed despite himself.

"Not likely, you crazy--!"

The woods were suddenly filled with terrifyingly shrill cries.

"Alce!" Baelor yelled, only to be answered with a shake of his head.

"I'm still too weak at the moment." His red eyes were trained on the redhead. "Daynel, use your recall spell!"

Her eyes were wide with fear. She whimpered before answering. "I-I don't know! Maybe…but it won't give us much distance!"

"It'll bring us closer to the horses, Lady Daynel," Rane informed her. He nodded appreciatively as she immediately began to chant her spell.

"Ah thought magyk ahttracted dem…?" Evergreen started, confused.

They all paused when Daynel motioned for Rane to drop her. She placed her hand on the ground and cried out, alarmed, as the spell failed to encircle all of them.

"No!" Daynel, Darec, and Rane vanished in a flash of flames, leaving everyone else.

Baelor grabbed his daughter from Tyrus, surprising the both of them.

"Change," he hissed to the boy. "Now!"

Tyrus looked at him in surprise. "Sire?"

"I know you can control it, change now and get my daughter out of here!" He watched as the boy nodded, removing his tunic with a swipe of rapidly lengthening claws.

Evergreen watched as Tyrus shredded his trousers, shedding them quickly before falling to all fours. Tyrus tripled in size, the freakish wolf they had gotten used to seeing replaced quickly by an even more monstrous wolf form. He had glowing violet eyes, large protruding fangs that pushed passed his thin lips. His fore body was mostly fur, wild and abysmal black intermingled with obsidian scales that gave off an iridescent sheen as they covered his hind quarters and tail before tapering into a razored point. Baelor tossed his daughter onto the wolf daemon's back and watched them speed off.

"This is a trap," Alce said.

"You knew she wouldn't get all of us, didn't you?" Zeph looked at the blond elf, who nodded.

"Sorry, but yes." He pulled out a pouch. "We're surrounded. The spell used to attract them--"

"Is mine."

They all looked around, the forest filled with chilling whoops and yips of the evil beasts that lived here. Baelor froze when he spied the owner first.

"It's been a long time, Baelor."

CHAPTER TWENTY

Feral

They were surrounded by goblins: squat with arms twice the length of their bodies; long, gangly fingers tipped with dirty, evil claws; fetid maws with jagged, yellow teeth. Sickly, yellow eyes partially hidden by matted, greenish-brown fur that covered frighteningly agile bodies. Goblins, the namesake of the woods they trespassed. Their maddening squeals filled the air coupled with their frantic scurrying as they pursued the warhorse-sized wolf and his dainty rider.

Tirin's neck ached as she strained to watch behind her despite the jarring of Tyrus' movements. She turned forward and regretted it, as her stomach didn't seem to care for the speed her 'steed' had. He darted in and out of trees, weaving back and forth, dodging not only trees but also the infrequent ax or arrow. She gripped his mane, apologizing for her tight hold as she buried her face into his neck.

By the droves, the squat hairy monsters appeared on either side of them. The goblins were clawing at her clothing, trying their hardest to separate her from him. Tyrus was no longer afraid of the little abominations; he was angry. Angry at their craftiness to gradually guide them away from camp. Angry with himself as there was nothing he could do about it, not alone. If he stopped they would attack without a doubt, but how long would they run him? He couldn't keep this pace for too much longer, not while carrying Tirin.

His concerns were short-lived, as Tirin screamed before Tyrus plowed head first into the ground with the weight of unwanted passengers. They were separated immediately.

Tirin's screams stabbed through him more viciously than any blade could before he was buried beneath the goblins' filthy weight. His sight was obscured by the number of monsters that piled on top of him. Tyrus disappeared, momentarily unable to free himself. Then her frantic cries caused him to go into a frenzy. He watched, unable to get away while seven of the monsters carried her off kicking and screaming. They piled on top of him again, biting him, gouging him, and ripping at his flesh as he struggled madly to free himself.

"*Tyrus!*" Tirin shrieked from somewhere deeper in the woods.

An anguished howl ripped free.

Gar watched the small group. "No questions? No threats?"

"Who are you?" Baelor growled out. "What do you want?"

Gar allowed a slow grin to creep across his face. "I am an old…acquaintance." He chuckled. "Not that it matters. My concern is not with any of you--"

An angry howl rent the air, causing Baelor to glare at the stranger. "You were after my daughter." His heart thumped in his chest angrily.

Gar raised his eyes to stare at Baelor in shock. "Your daughter?" He laughed. "Interesting, but indirectly."

"No!" Baelor shut his eyes tight. This couldn't be happening! "NO!

Gar stood calmly a few yards away from the reduced group. The Ferine, the wyld mage, a guard and Baelor. The old Imperial snarled and launched himself at the newcomer, but Zeph blocked him.

"He knows you, Sire," the old guard hissed before Baelor could snap at him. He calmed down quickly. He wanted to catch up with Tyrus, get his daughter. But Zeph had a point. The strange human knew him somehow. Had he been watched? That would be impossible; he hadn't left Ao'lean since returning all those years ago with Tirin. He studied the man's face; he was strangely familiar, but Baelor knew no other humans besides Zola and his former master, and that was long ago.

"Why?" Baelor asked with tight restraint, noticing how the goblins had now surrounded them.

Gar smirked. "Revenge."

"For?"

Gar laughed. "Pride? Jealousy? Hate? It doesn't really matter which you pick, they all work."

Alce stared at the human, unable to put his finger on why the man looked wrong. He carefully reached into the small pouch, his eyes stared at the horizon. Just a little longer.

"I don't know you, human--" Baelor started, only to pause as a face popped into his head, one he hadn't thought of in several decades. He shook it away, but Zeph nudged him.

"He looks like--"

"Ah, but you do, I've just changed...a bit. Don't worry, I don't hold it against you." Gar smirked. "At least not yet."

"Not yet?" Baelor snapped. "You're crazy. I have nothing to do with--"

"What happened to your pretty Loa?"

Zeph watched as the old Imperial stiffened in shock. How did this man know of Loa?

"I see you wear no marriage band; she must've died." His ice blue eyes stared into Baelor's brown ones. "Was it when you got a human wench pregnant?"

They didn't see Baelor move, but his target dodged the attack with the aid of his goblin lackeys. Two goblins lay on the ground, cleaved in two. Four more goblins stood in front of Gar, teeth and claws ready.

"Who are you?" Baelor thundered, pointing his gore-drenched blade at the strange human sorcerer. "What is your infatuation with my family?"

"That's enough," Gar started, only to watch as the wyld mage suddenly smiled.

"I agree." Alce threw the hand he had in his pouch up, flinging a fine dust into the air. Baelor and Zeph looked at the young elf like he was crazy.

"What is this?" Gar coughed and then pulled back, a motion that caused the surrounding goblins to move forward threateningly. Alce winked at the 'human'.

"An accident." Quickly, Evergreen grabbed Zeph's and Baelor's hands.

Gar watched, startled, as the young elf's eyes turned pitch black. "Kill them," Gar said coldly. The goblins became frenzied.

Before anyone moved, the first rays of the sun climbed over the horizon, causing the dust to sparkle fantastically, setting the air seemingly on fire. It was then that Gar realized that the powder had yet to fall. Without pause he quickly covered his eyes.

The glittering dust shone brightly, growing in intensity before absorbing every bit of light and causing a darkness so deep that the goblins squealed in utter fear. Their collective thought was that the smaller yellow-haired elf had somehow banished the sun.

Suddenly blind, Gar stood still, listening as his four prisoners made their escape using the Ferine's unique second sight.

Zeph and Baelor followed blindly as Evergreen led them through the strange darkness.

"What was that?" Zeph asked in amazement when they emerged from the darkness almost as abruptly as it had appeared.

Alce smiled broadly. "An accident I created a couple of years ago that has finally found use."

Baelor inspected the giant globe of darkness behind them. It was impenetrable by the rising sun, a black hole in the middle of the air.

"Will they be able to get out of there?" he asked quietly.

Alce smirked. "Depends. The goblins probably think me some kind of God now so they probably won't dare to move." He scratched his head.

"But what about the human? He's not as simple-minded." Baelor started to turn back. "I say we kill him now."

"No!" Evergreen snapped. "We must find Tirin and Tyrus!"

Baelor looked at her, torn. He needed to check on his daughter and the boy, but couldn't stomach the thought that the sorcerer was after her. "He'll find a way out and come after her."

"It'll take too long to find him in that darkness. As for the supposed 'human'--"

Both Baelor and Zeph looked at Alce. "Supposed?"

***

Daynel fell to the ground once the spell ended. Her hysterical crying reduced her to an immobile heap. Rane quickly stood her up.

"They'll be all right, Lady. Don't worry, they ain't weak folks."

"Unlike me," she whimpered. He held her, brushing her hair from her face.

"Let's get the horses."

They rushed to the horses tied beyond the now ruined campsite. Mounting quickly, they suddenly realized too late that someone was missing.

"Where--?" Rane started, looking where Daynel was pointing behind him. They watched as the mad Lord rode off on his horse.

225

They remained still for a moment and watched while he disappeared into the forest.

"Should we chase after him?" Daynel asked, hoping that the answer was no.

Rane shook his head, to the redhead's relief. "Nah, one less nut to worry about. Let's get back to the others."

Daynel gulped.

The flames of the recall spell weakened the rope binding Darec. The Young Lord didn't waste time trying to determine how. He had to get away before they realized he was free.

He'd get his revenge eventually. Necrom whinnied, alarmed, when he snatched the horse's reins sharply, catching Daynel's attention. He narrowed his eyes at her. She would be the first to pay.

***

They moved quickly toward camp, hoping to run into the others. The large globe of night slowly expanded behind them. Only a little time was lost due to their convincing Baelor not to go back in to kill the strange sorcerer. They had to find Tirin and Tyrus.

"What do you mean, 'supposed'?" Baelor moved closer to the wizard. Alce simply shrugged.

"His appearance was what attracted the goblins." He jumped over a downed sapling. "Goblins are attracted to magyk, but it has to be a certain type of magyk. They don't like creation magyk." He watched them look at him in confusion.

"Magyk is magyk," Zeph said.

"Typical. No. Creation magyk happens naturally. Air, earth, water, and so on; these they hate. But magyk that changes the nature of an object." Alce waved his hand toward the forest. "They worship that stuff."

"So?" Zeph panted.

Baelor eyed the guard with slight irritation. He was older by at least fifty years and he had yet to feel any strain. "The goblins have no leadership. They follow anyone who can transform things--"

"Or people," Alce finished. "But you've got to prove yourself."

Baelor looked ahead of them; they should be nearing the campsite soon. "Will he be able to get out of your spell?"

"Only if he has a good sense of direction. The darkness is not stationary; believe me, I know." Evergreen smirked at Alce, recalling how his experiment had engulfed the hovel. Bayne hadn't been happy. "He can't cast any light spells or fire spells; the dust absorbs light, any light."

"Theey herded him away," Evergreen suddenly stated.

Baelor stopped immediately. The other two came to a stop behind him. They watched as Evergreen knelt down and touched the trampled ground.

"We will run eento ah horde of the beasties." She paused and looked toward where camp was. They all eventually heard the sound of hooves heading their way. Warily the four braced themselves just in case. The bright red of Daynel's hair clued them in on to who was approaching.

"Did you see them?" Baelor asked when the two came to a stop, hoping that Tyrus would have been able to redirect himself.

Without pause, Rane could see that Tyrus and Tirin must have been sent away soon after they disappeared. But something went wrong. He shook his head.

"They did not come this way."

Evergreen quickly mounted her horse and headed back the way they came.

"Where is she going?" Daynel asked, confused. Before Alce could answer, the Ferine yelled back.

"This way!"

None of them wasted time. Following the Ferine's voice, they caught up with her.

"What happened to the Young Lord?" Alce asked from behind Daynel. He watched as she cringed a bit.

"He got away. I think my spell may have--"

She watched his eyes turn blue. "We'll work on your focus."

***

Resembling a dark apparition in her flowing dark green cloak, the woman floated through the swamp silently. The frown on her face deepened as she passed over several downed trees.

That boy was nothing but trouble. She quietly landed upon the front porch and immediately was hit with the scent of wet dog.

"What in the twelve hells---?" she complained before entering the small hovel. The scent intensified and she could see that the dog had fought tooth and nail against Alce before more than likely succumbing to that charm of his. The claw marks stretched across the floor planks and into the main spell room. "I hope he doesn't think I'm going to allow him a pet after all this time."

Bayne smirked as she scanned the shelved walls. Their many books, vials and concoctions were missing, on this plane of existence anyway. Alce did pay attention; he wasn't as incompetent as he let on.

She glided over to the largest of the four tables in the main room. On it stood a tiny vial of crimson. Blood.

She waved her hand and the vial vanished. In its place was a rather odd-looking wolf that quickly changed into a tall elven boy who stood proudly in miniature form on the table. Bayne cocked her head to the side. She knew this boy.

Fingering the familiar necklace about her throat, she wracked her brain for a reason why the boy was so familiar to her. Slowly it came to her.

There weren't many visitors to this dismal swamp, and even fewer elves. But this one had the audacity to try and steal from her. Just as she was about to smile at the memory of the young elf's attempt so long ago, the necklace about her neck grew suddenly ice cold. Bayne stood there, rigid, almost unable to react as she hadn't felt anything from the heirloom in years.

Her sister's necklace was calling out to hers. Bayne rushed out of the hovel to stand on the porch. All these years and the necklace never did a thing. What was happening now to cause such fear?

"Show me." Her voice barely a whisper and yet echoed through the night.

Slowly the air swirled before her, gradually forming a picture of a dark-skinned girl running across the balcony of what appeared to be a palace. Around the girl's neck bounced her family's heirloom.

"Zola had a daughter." Only blood relatives could wear that necklace. Bayne found herself almost jealous and yet still wary. The girl was so big! She had to be almost a woman from the look of her.

The way she was running told her that the girl was in trouble. Pride filled her as her sister's child promised to be a Terra-witch like herself. Bayne watched the girl hurl bolts of lightning and gales of vicious wind at her pursuers before witnessing the largest fire-wheel she had ever seen conjured. It was a wonder the girl didn't black out from the amount of energy needed for such a spell, especially for a novice her age. The girl needed training, but she was strong. It pained her to see her niece in such a predicament.

Bayne started to cast a summoning spell when she saw the boy whose blood was on her table. Partially transformed, the boy made his way over to her weakened niece, who was more than excited to see him.

That's when she noticed the small signs of the girl's heritage. She was half elf!

What had Zola done? Who was she with and where was she now? The picture faded and she turned back into the hovel.

The girl was going to be powerful with the right training. Bayne's worry over her bloodline coming to an end was now irrelevant. She recalled the look on the elven boy's face. He loved her.

But where in the world were Alce and Evergreen?

***

The smell of the goblins' burning flesh and fur was horrendous. It burned in her nose and throat, making it even harder for her to catch her breath as she ran. It was in her clothes and hair. Two of them had exploded when she cast that haphazard lightning spell. Tirin cried out as one of the little monsters jumped out of the bushes at her. They were toying with her, purposely leading her further and further away from Tyrus and her father. Her mind kept going back to seeing them pile on Tyrus, and the fact that she had no idea what her father and the others were going through. She was close to hysterics, unable to get herself to calm down. She tripped suddenly and went flying into a bush. The goblins jumped on her, tearing at her clothes and hair. She snapped.

***

The metallic scent of blood filled the air. The ripping of flesh along with squeals of pain and terror became maddening the closer they got. The bodies of goblins littered the ground, giving them a gory trail to follow. They dismounted quietly.

Baelor cautioned them while they continued forward toward the vicious growling. They found a sight none of them were expecting. The lupine monster stood on two legs. Blood-filled jaws crushed the neck of one victim while claws ripped into another.

The elves silently stood back and watched, too shocked to move and more than a little afraid to call Tyrus' attention while he continued to fight to free himself from the small horde.

One of the goblins noticed the other elves and squealed in alarm. The attacking mass pulled away from Tyrus, heading back into the woods and leaving the enraged beast panting behind them.

Zeph watched, amazed yet again, as Tyrus' form shrank in on itself, becoming smaller yet still larger than a normal wolf. The boy's legs trembled before dropping him to the ground. Rather quickly the fur melted into bloodied skin. His body was covered with weeping lacerations and darkening bruises. Tyrus remained still, almost too still, worrying Baelor.

"Tyrus—?" Baelor started and stopped when abruptly the boy's crazed eyes locked onto them. He growled and snapped viciously, baring his fangs in warning. The elves braced themselves.

Tyrus panted heavily before forcing himself back to his feet. Ignoring the smell of his own blood, he howled mournfully. He shifted quickly back into the monstrous wolf and then bounded off behind the retreating goblins.

Baelor sighed.

"Shouldn't we--?" Rane started only to watch Baelor shake his head.

"Let him go."

Alce looked at the ground, not sure what to do next. He looked at his companion. Evergreen shook her head as well, "He's gone feral, but he'll find her."

*****

I hope you've enjoyed the first half of Wonderlost! The story
will continue in the next book: Reunions
Until then, thanks so much for your support of indie authors
and giving me the chance to entertain you!
Keep in touch!
AntoinetteHouston.com
@1975Okame on Twitter
www.facebook.com/RedSummerUF

Antoinette J. Houston